ALSO BY ASH LINGAM

I0534721

To Hell and Back

Unwanted Reunion

RUN FOR YOUR LIFE

RUN FOR YOUR LIFE

JED & JODIE DESPERADOS
BOOK 3

ASH LINGAM

WISE WOLF
BOOKS

WISE WOLF BOOKS
An Imprint of Wolfpack Publishing
wisewolfbooks.com
1707 E. Diana Street
Tampa, FL 33610

Paperback ISBN 978-1-965596-07-4
eBook ISBN 978-1-965596-06-7

This book is dedicated to Tikotta Horse Refuge located in Canyelles, Spain in the province of Barcelona. It is a profit-free organization for homeless and abandoned horses.

"Good news is rare these days, and every glittering ounce of it should be cherished and hoarded and worshipped and fondled like a priceless diamond."

—Hunter S. Thompson

PREFACE

Jed Coal and John Washington were inducted into Captain William Quantrill's Raiders through no choice of their own. Coal, a young White man, was recruited from the ordinary Confederate army because of his sharpshooting skills. Washington was an enslaved Black man who was loaned to the notorious captain. He became Jed's spotter and mentor, and they managed to survive the war together.

When the war ended, those of Quantrill's Raiders who survived fled Missouri and rode south to friendlier locations. Every soldier, sheriff, and marshal in the country was on their trail. The captain met his end in Tennessee as he tried to reach his home in Canner Dover, Ohio. Others, like the James brothers and the Youngers, rode in different directions.

Jed and John split from the more zealous compatriots and fled for Texas.

Jodi Goodnight was the niece of the famous rancher Charles Goodnight. She was a tomboy as a child and grew up with her father's ranch hands. As she reached adulthood, her riding and shooting skills were superior to all but her father. When he died, and the bank repossessed their ranch a piece at a time, Jodi was left to survive on her own.

Due to her pride, she disfigured a man for life when he made a lude pass at her. Unfortunately, he was the town sheriff, and now she was on the run, too. It was not long before fate threw Jodi together with Jed and John. Neither wanted to have the extra baggage, nor entwine her in their criminal behavior, which sometimes included the likes of the James brothers, Frank and Jesse. Who knew there was an affair in store for the unlikely couple? Would her association with the ex-Raiders' problems claim her life, too?

RUN FOR YOUR LIFE

CHAPTER 1

CRIME OF COLOR

MOMENTS BEFORE, JOHN WASHINGTON HAD FELT AS HAPPY as a pig at a morning feed. He was wallowing in the delight of being a free man. That changed when his old companions — the James brothers and Cole Younger — showed up, and he remembered who he was. He wasn't going to be what he dreamed. This was as free as he was going to get. The freedom Black folks would feel in the future was something he would never experience. He was happy he had gotten a taste of what it might be like, though.

Since the James Gang arrived in El Paso, John felt more paranoid with each passing minute. Here he sat at a table with three of Captain William. Quantrill's Raiders while half the country was looking for them. Everybody was after Jesse since the day he turned sixteen and he joined Bloody Bill Anderson's Marauders back in Missouri.

After the Centralia Massacre, the young boy was never the same. It was the most sinister and brutal battle of the Civil War. Bloody Bill ordered his men to murder unarmed Union soldiers and take scalps, ears, and even noses. Some said he was a brilliant strategist, putting his eighty men against three times those numbers time and again and coming out victorious. Those who rode with him knew he was a psychopath, using the war as an excuse to kill, mutilate and defile.

The day he was finally shot from his horse, Jesse and Frank James were with him. They barely got away from Glasgow, Kentucky, with their lives.

Washington and his partner, Jed Coal, saw Jesse's face on the front pages of newspapers when they visited the occasional town. Washington couldn't read, but he knew they only put the faces of infamous outlaws on the first page. He had no problem with numbers, though. There was more money in bounties sitting at the table than in the in the safes of some banks.

"Come on, John. You can tell an old pard," Jesse coaxed his war buddy. "Whose idea was it to rob two banks at once? And who in the world thought up stealing the whole danged train? I don't take kindly to being showed up." He winked because Jesse was in a good mood today, which was lucky for John and everybody else.

"It was Jed and me who decided to rob both the banks on the same morning. We'd watched 'em for a few days, deciding which one to hit. Then we figured why not have a go at 'em both and head for the train. It was Jodi's idea to steal the locomotive. A clever one, she is. She conned the engineer to teach her to run it and then booted him and the fireman out and stole it. We only had to stop for water, but Jodi kept a gun to his ribs, and nobody found anything different than any other day. It went off as slick as spit."

"When we left the passengers, Jodi threw the throttle to full speed, setting the train into motion. Then she jumped off, and we wheeled our horses for safety. The locomotive chugged all the way to Harrisburg before it ran out of steam and water—it also ran out of track and ran aground; there was no one to stop it," John said, stopping for a moment to stifle a laugh. "They say it took the railroad until the next day to figure out where the passengers were. Fancy folks don't take to walking, especially wearing city shoes. The first day the train arrived without the passengers, the newspapers said it was a ghost train. Those rags jump at the first lie that comes to mind."

"I must admit, y'all got gumption," Frank said with a smile.

"I doubt I'd be so brash iff'n I was alone," John Washington grinned.

Suddenly they heard heavy boots on the saloon porch. Then the batwing doors burst open with a bang. The sheriff stood on the threshold as his three deputies backed him up. All of them had guns pointed at the Black man. Frank and Cole went tense, but Jesse just smiled. John froze. At that range, there was no way they'd miss.

"That's the murderin' dog right there," the sheriff shouted as his deputies rushed up behind him.

"Is your name John Washington, mister?" Sheriff Gibbons asked as he pointed a revolver at his head.

John's eyes shifted from Frank to Coal, then to Jesse. The younger James brother was just about to sass the sheriff. John could sense it. He'd known Jesse for too long and knew how much he hated the law. He didn't want a shootout in a saloon full of innocent bystanders, though. It wasn't worth it to the Black man.

John put a hand on Jesse's arm, took his feet and said, "Yes, sir, Sheriff. I be John Washington."

"Grab 'em, boys. Be careful now, though," Gibbons said. "He's already killed and robbed the fella in the alley. Come along, or I'll shoot ya where ya stand."

They accused John of murder. He thought, for sure, there would be bloodshed. The lawman didn't recognize the other outlaws at the table, though. They were too excited about the prospect of hanging somebody — especially a Negro.

John was arrested for the murder of a town citizen. Nobody said a thing about the Raiders or Missouri. A strange Black man with money in town wasn't a normal occurrence, and somebody pointed him out, and immediately everybody assumed he was the culprit. How else would he have so much cash? They easily discovered his name from the hotel registry.

Frank, Jesse, and Cole let their gun hands slip under the table. But John didn't want a gunfight in the middle of a saloon, even if he had Jesse James on his side. He'd caused enough killing. The sheriff, of course, apprehended the wrong man. John was a killer; he just hadn't killed anyone in El Paso. The authorities had no idea of how much of a killer he actually was.

Jesse went to stand again, but Frank put a hand on his shoulder and whispered, "Don't worry, John. As soon as Jed gets back, we'll deal with this."

For the briefest of moments, the sheriff gave the three men a questioning look. He could feel the danger come off them in waves—like heat from a bonfire. Their presence made him nervous for some reason, so his mind immediately turned back to the prospect of a lynching. It made him feel good again; perhaps he would be elevated to hero status.

He let the other men at the table slip his mind and said, "The Negro goes with me. I'm the town law." His voice didn't sound as brave as he had hoped. "I've got no problem with y'all, but I'm afraid I'm gonna have to take the Black man with me."

Frank James nodded and kept his grip on his brother's shoulder. Jesse and John had their differences occasionally, but the four had fought together through the Civil War. It created a special bond, especially among men who rode with Quantrill's Raiders. No, sir, this was not over by a long shot.

John only hoped Jed and Jodi would come back sooner rather than later. If they tried to hang him, he knew there would be bloodshed. Jesse wouldn't be able to resist. To everybody in town, he was just another Black man whose death would be little to no consequence. Only his friends and brothers from Missouri—members of Quantrill's Raiders and Anderson's Marauders—would care.

WHEN JED and Jodi packed their things and saddled their horses to leave, it was apparent neither one wanted to depart. It was such a peaceful place, and they were the only people around. It was their first time alone for more than a few hours. Nobody was chasing them and, for a moment, they felt like two ordinary lovers.

Jed slept with his pistol under the saddle and never left it out of reach, but his eyes weren't as hollow as before. If given the time and opportunity, Jodi believed she could heal his wounds and help him live at peace with himself. She didn't know how serious his injuries were or how red his blood ran. She was willing to try, though.

They rode back into El Paso, like always, with some trepidation. Just because things appeared normal, didn't mean they were. They wheeled their horses toward the hotel, where John said he would meet them. It was a two-story building with large decorative columns on the front. The sign at the top said Peaceful Hotel. Jodi saw the name and smiled.

Maybe their vacation from all the danger and death wasn't over, she thought.

"Let's have a drink before we get a room," Jed said as they stopped in front of the hotel. He kicked his leg over his horn and slid off the saddle with his hand on his pistol grip. "I'd like to check things out before we check in."

When they pushed open the batwing doors, their eyes had to get used to the dim light of eight kerosene lamps with the wicks turned down. It was an elegant saloon with a few gentlemen engaged in card games. Jed's eyes swept the room.

"When are you ever going to relax a little?" Jodi asked. "You see ghosts where most folks see people."

They walked into the tavern, holding hands. Jed immediately squeezed Jodi tight without realizing he was hurting her. Jodi's eyes followed him to the corner of the bar. There sat Frank James in the corner, and it looked like his brother, Jesse, was with him. They were sitting with a man Jodi didn't recognize, but Jed did.

Jed's heart jumped to his throat and his pulse raced.

His eyes took in the whole room, but there was no sign of John Washington, his war partner. A bad feeling drifted like a storm cloud over his soul.

The afternoon was humid; it felt swampy and as thick as summer. The saloon had two large windows on either side, but the curtains hung limp without the slightest breeze. The room closed in on Jed as his vision pinpointed to the table in the corner.

"What now, Jed?" Jodi whispered. "We can always turn around and walk out."

He heard words, but his mind was elsewhere. For a moment, he was back in the war. He had fought and saw friends die with the three men at the table. When Frank nodded his head, and Jesse turned around, they didn't smile. Their eyes were filled with violence. Jed immediately knew something had happened to John. He felt it in his gut. He roared across the room with Jodi, trying to keep up.

"Where ya goin' so fast?" Jodi barked but Jed ignored her.

"Where's John?" Jed immediately asked.

"A how do you do might be in order," Jesse growled playfully. But Jed knew him well; he was just blowing wind. His eyes held concern.

"Hush up for once," Frank said. Jesse got a sharp look from his brother, but he ignored him as usual. "We were sitting at the table by the door. We'd just come into town, and there was John. We all sat down together, and after a spell, in came a sheriff. He said John robbed and murdered a man."

"I wanted to shoot 'em dead right then and there," Jesse spat and made the sign of the cross. "But Frank wouldn't let me."

"John had no need to steal, and I'm sure if he killed somebody, he wouldn't hang around for a sheriff to arrest him," Jed said. "Where's he now?"

"That was three days ago, Jed," Jesse said. "He's due for a hearing in court today. We were all goin' over and, depending on the verdict, plan to see what we can do to bust him out. Don't worry, pardner. They ain't going to hang one of us Raiders unless they hang us all."

Frowning, Jed plopped down and his brow furrowed. The bartender brought another glass. He filled it with whiskey and turned the glass up. Then he remembered Jodi. He looked back, and there she stood with arms crossed and her hip kicked out. Her mouth was a hard line.

She stormed up to the table and declared, "Don't y'all ignore me like that, especially you, Jed. Whatcha doin'? Did you forget I was here as soon as we got back?"

She'd never talked to him like that before, but he decided to bite his tongue until he had a chance to see what this was all about.

"The sheriff arrested John for robbery and murder," Jed said to the angry woman.

Jody's demeanor changed abruptly. She had begun to consider John as a kind of uncle. He and Jed were all the family she had. She forgot her petty anger and focused on the problem.

CHAPTER 2

COURTHOUSE CHAOS

JOHN ENTERED THE COURTROOM WITH IRON SHACKLES around his ankles. They rattled against the floorboards as he shuffled his way to the front. He kept his eyes glued to the floor, just like Black people in the South did before abolition.

By the time his friends entered the courtroom, some spectators already were yelling: "Hang 'em until he's dead."

Another gawker yelled, "Let's take 'em out and string 'em up him now!"

When the jurors filed in and took their seats, they had half-moons of sweat under their arms. The room was filled with disgruntled citizens who only wanted to see a Black man swing. Their protests became so loud it was impossible to hear what anybody said.

A tall, lanky judge pushed his way through a door behind the bench. He had a large head, a sardonic smile and his eyes betrayed his agitation. His black robe fluttered behind him. As his head turned, he perched his raven-like figure on the bench and gazed into the crowd.

He made no effort to hide his scorn and distaste for those present.

The judge wielded his gavel with such fury it looked like he might smash a hole in his hickory top.

Bam! Bam! Bam!

His Honor scowled over the rim of his glasses and stared the audience down. He intimidated the courtroom into silence.

Jed studied the faces of the jurors before turning to his longtime partner. Then he forced a smile.

"What's the Black man accused of?" the judge immediately asked the prosecuting attorney.

"Murder, of course! How else would a Black man have enough money to dine in the best restaurant in town?" the lawyer replied.

The lawyer for the prosecution was a skillful actor. When it came to talking, he was a magician with words. He took the jury down the dark alley where someone butchered the victim with a knife and stole his money. He detailed the gory assault as he imagined the crime. He wanted the jury to feel the fear of the victim. The only stranger of color in town was the Black man, who claimed to be John Washington. He also appeared to be wealthy.

Jed and Jodi sat in a pew three rows back. Cole Younger and the James brothers sat right behind them. Jed looked back and saw where their hidden pistols bulged under their jackets. All of the courtroom was focused on the accused.

Even though Washington wore fine clothing he bought in San Antonio, his face couldn't hide his history of violence. The scars were there for everyone to see. Among the jury, a few women nearly fainted when John looked their way. Despite a lack of evidence and no witnesses, the attorney wanted the jury to believe John was guilty just because he had money and was black. The latter was the primary motivator.

John looked at it from a philosophical point of view. If the truth was known, Washington had committed more crimes than he could count. Some were with the Marauder before the war in Kansas. Others were after the war with Jed and the Raiders. He felt if he wasn't guilty of one thing; he was guilty of a hundred others. He was ready to face the music. For a small window in time, he had experienced freedom. He hoped his brother would enjoy freedom one day, too.

The prosecution slowly stood, walked around his desk and picked up a tattered Bible. He flipped through the pages, looking for a verse from the book of Proverbs he had memorized but acted as though he had just stumbled upon the passage.

"When justice is done, it brings joy to the righteous!" he admonished the jury. Then he *slammed* the Bible closed to make a point, startling the female jurors.

He went on to portray John as a black demon. As far as Jed could see, it was the fact that John dressed in fine duds that riled him so. It didn't matter who killed and robbed the drunk in the alley beside the saloon. Some saw a sassy, highfalutin Negro and decided he was the perpetrator of the crime. Apparently, it provided and easy excuse to hang a Black man.

Like a fever, there had been lynchings all across the South since the war's end. Some folks thought they were getting even; others just did it to appease their lust for violence. The Civil War left a scar across the country that ran so deep it might never completely heal.

Finally, it was the defense attorney's turn to make a stand. He walked around the table as he buttoned the top button on his shirt and then pulled up his string tie. He brushed his straight black hair from his face and nodded accusingly at each member seated in the jury box.

"So, there it is," the barrister declared. "He's a Negro! Do you all agree with this fact, ladies and gentlemen of the jury?"

Puzzled by his approach, they all nodded their heads. Of course, they knew he was a Negro.

"And you, ladies and gentlemen, are all White. Am I correct again?"

Like before, the jurors nodded in unison, more confused than ever.

"We all knew what a Negro and a White man look like, young man," the judge roared. "Do you take us for country fools? You best get to it if you're trying to make a point."

"Everybody expects a White jury to convict a Black man," the defense attorney stated. "Is there not a man or woman among you who does not have the integrity, or a smidgen of honor left? Here we have a man accused of the worst crime against humanity—murder. No, it was more like an assassination."

The defending attorney looked across the faces of the jury as he nodded his head accusingly.

"But let me ask you a few simple questions. Do we have a murder weapon? No, we do not. Do we have a motive? Not based on the way Mr. Washington dresses."

"I doubt the twenty dollars stolen from…" The counselor paused to check his notes before continuing. "…Mr. Gerald Jones would be enough to buy John Washington's hat.

"Did they pass a law when they freed the enslaved people that said a Black man was forbidden to have money? Has there been any prior instance where Mr. Washington assaulted or even spoke to someone other than a bartender to request a drink? Was our client inebriated, I ask? No, he was not. He was sitting with three fine, White gentlemen, who are present in the courtroom today. Still, the district attorney accuses him of murder on hearsay evidence. Need I say more?"

The courtroom exploded with exception, drowning out an ugly smattering of applause. They began to chant: "String him up! String him up!"

A sly smile flashed across the judge's face before he managed to swallow it. He didn't do it fast enough for Jed or the James Gang not to notice, though. They knew right then that the court intended to hang John for something he did not do; it mattered little what the defense said.

Jesse James stood and yelled, "Hey, fancy pants!"

The younger James brother pulled his gun and shot the prosecutor in the heart. He looked down unbelievingly as a red stain raced across his white shirt. Color drained from his face. Suddenly, his knees buckled and he fell to one side, finally sliding to the floor with a thud. Blood pooled beneath his body. The judge went for the revolver that sat beside his mallet, but Jodi was quicker with her six-gun. It bucked once, blowing a hole in His Honor's hand.

Jed stood, aimed two Colt Walkers at the sheriff and his deputy. "Take those chains off, my friend right now!" he ordered.

The sheriff frowned and began to protest. Jed drew back the hammers on his revolvers and the click of the chambers was enough for the town law to understand he was knocking at heaven's door. He fumbled with the keys and, with the help of the deputy, freed John.

"I don't take kindly to men who put my friends in chains," Jed said right before shooting the sheriff in the kneecap. He howled like a wolf in a steel trap.

"Are you ready, Deputy?" he asked.

He shook his head and said, "You don't have to shoot me too, do ya?"

"You locked my friend up in those chains and planned to hang him, didn't ya?"

Jed shot him in his right shoulder, spinning him like a top. He crashed across a table.

"Now, I reckon you both be out of a job. You won't be walking for a year and you deputy won't be aiming that gun at another man unless it be with his left hand," Jed calmly said.

"Come on, boys!" Jesse yelled as he shot out the lights and windows. His bullets whizzed wildly through the air. More glass shattered and wood splintered. Everybody, including the judge, dove for the safety of the floor.

"That'll teach y'all to try to lock up one of the James Gang," Jesse yelled.

Jody and Jed grabbed John and followed the rest of Quantrill's Raiders out of the courtroom. Their horses were waiting outside. A flurry of hooves hammered the street and corkscrewed dust into the air. The desperados quickly disappeared into the distance until they were no more than silhouettes on the horizon.

The people in the courtroom kept their heads down for several minutes after the outlaws fled. The sheriff rolled on the floor with his hands holding his shattered knee. His deputy passed out from the pain as blood soaked his gray shirt.

Would the deputy be lefthanded from now on? Would the sheriff walk with a limp for the rest of his life? If they were clever, they would save the bullets for bragging rights. Slugs from the famous Jesse James could make them celebrities, even though they would have to retire. At least it would keep them in free drinks every time they told the tale. Getting shot by Jesse James and surviving was something few men could claim.

CHAPTER 3

THE POSSE

WHEN THE SHOOTING STOPPED, THE PEOPLE IN THE courtroom were still under benches, tables, and pews, anywhere they could escape the flying bullets. Jesse James was a man nobody wanted to cross. Many places in the South thought he and his brother were heroes. Some of his closest friends knew differently, though. Jesse was rotten to the core, a product of his environment. In Missouri, years before the Civil War, violence erupted on the Kansas border. His father, a Baptist pastor, drummed it into young Jesse's head the South was right and all others were wrong. Violence was the only answer.

After the war, survivors of Quantrill's Raiders scattered to the wind and became wanted men with no future. So, they turned to crime and violence, something they embraced like a brother. Robbing banks and trains was their specialty.

The five outlaws fled south of the border and its relative safety. The James Gang was already notorious across the country; bounty hunters dreamed of claiming the money on their heads. Jed and John had successfully avoided getting mixed up with their old war buddies. They were looking for something else in life instead of more of the same war they had just spent years fighting. Plus, they knew if they were tied to the James Gang, they would be more wanted than they were already.

Jodi was yet to be identified, although Jed Coal and John Washington were known to be on the run with a blonde White woman who could ride and shoot like a man. Nobody had figured out who she was yet. Just being a Goodnight would mean the news would make the headlines unless John and Jed could avoid allowing her identity to be divulged. As they rode south, their chances of doing that just kept getting slimmer.

"GET THE MARSHAL OVER HERE, and I mean now!" Judge Axel Black roared at the wounded sheriff. He continued to roll on the courtroom floor, and his deputy was still unconscious and bleeding.

"Somebody call the doctor for Pete's sake," the judge spat. "How hard can it be to do something as simple as hanging a Black man? We're in the South, ain't we? Ya can't get no farther south than Texas."

The marshal was already on his way when he had heard the gunfire. He hadn't attended the hearing for two reasons. One, he wasn't the man who made the arrest and knew it was a bad habit to stick your nose in other people's business. Second, he knew they would hang an innocent man no matter what he said. So, he stayed in his office and out of sight. He never asked to be appointed to the six-gun capital of the world anyway.

Why should he risk his life with the likes of El Paso citizens? He wanted no part in the hanging.

Judge Black had his belt wrapped around his wrist to stem the bleeding. A gaping hole was visible where his palm used to be. He was so angry his courtroom had been violated he ignored the pain. He held his Colt revolver in his left fist as blue vein pulsated at his temple. Several more popped out on his neck. He was beside himself with anger by the time the marshal walked into the saloon.

Marshal Billy Bob Thorn cautiously walked up to the front of the tavern. He pushed his way through the crowd already gathered outside. His star flashed in the sunlight as he grasped his pistol in his right fist. He had no idea what he was walking into and wanted to be sure he had his weapon handy if things went south.

When Thorn heard several people in the crowd mention the names Jesse and Frank James, his blood turned to ice. His worst fears just walked right into his town, and there wasn't a dang thing he could do about it. As marshal, he would lead a posse after the James Gang. He thought he had run into bad luck a year back when they transferred him from quiet Laredo to El Paso. Now, his luck just turned to manure as sure as the judge was in the Ku Klux Klan's newly formed militia. Thorn stayed out of politics and never took sides, especially in a matter which caused the country to tear itself apart during the Civil War. For a proper lawman, politics could never be involved, he believed.

In 1865, those unhappy with the war's outcome joined secret and not-so-secret sects that fought against the abolition of slavery. Judge Black was one of them. He was the Klan's leader for all of Texas. For the judge to pursue the James brothers, who shared the same sentiments, seemed odd.

Marshal Thorn had worn the badge for nearly twenty years and had seen enough to know when things were about to get terribly dangerous. He could feel it in the crowd. It could turn into an unruly mob in seconds if something wasn't done. Then again, he knew from the mumbles Jesse and Frank James had just left the courthouse. That alone was enough to rile up any city. He needed to find out what happened inside.

"Step aside, now," Thorn ordered. "The law's coming through."

The crowd separated, making a path like parting seas. The marshal pushed the swinging doors open, hung his hands on the tops and looked across the room. He sucked on his quid and spat a yard of brown juice onto the porch before he entered. Somewhat calmed, the judge turned his way. His face was ashen white with shock. The pain showed in his face as Doc Adams wrapped the gaping wound the best he could. The judge knew he could lose the hand if he was unlucky. It wouldn't be of much use to him anymore anyway.

By the time the marshal arrived, the deputy was dead. His heart couldn't bear the stress caused by his wound and loss of blood. Thorn reached over and put two fingers to his carotid artery. The deputy's pulse was gone, and his body already was going cold. To make matters worse, it turned out three more innocent bystanders were wounded by bullets Jesse wildly tossed hither and thither like a madman. There wasn't a window in the courtroom that was unbroken. In his state of pain and shock, the judge still seethed as he looked at his courtroom in shambles.

Marshal Thorn felt somebody approaching from the rear. He spun on his heels and pulled his gun. Dr. Carl Adams nearly fainted on the spot when a big black barrel was pointed at his face.

"Sorry, Doc," Thorn said, "but you should know better than to sneak up on a man at a shootin'. How many bystanders here got hit? I heard a passel of guns go off."

"I count six wounded and one dead, countin' Judge Black here." He looked at the deputy on the floor and said, "Make that five wounded and two dead."

"Everybody not shot, get up and get out of my courtroom right now. Scat, dagnabbit!" Judge Black bellowed as Adams continued to work on his hand again. "Those shot, raise your hands iff'n ya ain't dead or dyin'."

People came out from under the furniture like termites in a fire. They couldn't get out of the saloon fast enough. The wounded even tried to sneak off, but Doc Adams responded quickly. Not a soul got away. Of course, the deputy wasn't going anywhere unless they got him into a wheelbarrow and carted him over to the funeral parlor and finally up to Boot Hill. Marshal Thorn squatted down, unpinned his star, and rifled the deputy's pockets.

The marshal stood, opened his palm to view a ring, two bits and a plug of tobacco. There was nothing left to give his relatives if anyone knew who they were or where they were located. Many men lived on names other than their own in the West, including lawmen. Half the marshals west of the Missouri River had been in hot water at some time in the past. Some changed their names as often as they shed their clothing. They did it whenever it was convenient.

Half the lawmen west of the Missouri were outlaws before they were lawmen, including famous men like Wyatt Earp and Wild Bill Hickok. Were they lawmen or guns for hire? Billy Bob figured a little of both.

Marshal Thorn grabbed the back of a chair and dragged it across the barroom floor and onto the porch. The mob parted like he had the plague. Billy Bob stepped up onto the chair, so he was heads above the crowd. He got no response when he held up his hand for quiet. So he pulled a Remington revolver and fired two rounds into the air. The citizens suddenly became silent.

"Y'all saw who done it well enough," Thorn blared. "I was told Jesse James identified himself. Some of you were probably friends of the deputy and the wounded citizens, not to mention Judge Black. Evil men have defiled your town. They took the lives of two of your own. Now, it's my job to track these men down, and bring 'em back here to serve justice. Judge Black ain't gonna be happy until we do. So, who is gonna go with me?"

Most of the men dropped their eyes to the toes of their boots to avoid eye contact with Marshal Thorn. Some simply turned and scurried away, leaving a small wake of dust as they fled. A few men exchanged looks with the marshal. They were angry and defiant, but there was a trace of fear there too.

"Do you think we don't know how dangerous Jesse and Frank James are?" Rap Ressie, a town businessman, asked. "We don't get paid to hunt down dangerous outlaws. Especially not the James Gang."

"Then I'll pay ya for your services," Marshal Thorn replied. "I'll deputize the lot of ya. How about them apples?"

"You ain't got enough cash for me to run after the likes of the James brothers. A dead man can't spend money," Ressie spat. "I ain't a coward, but I've never professed to be a hero either. You weren't here; you didn't see Jesse's eyes when he killed the lawyer. They were as wicked as I've ever seen. He laughed when he shot him, too. If I never see that devil's eyes again, it'll be too danged soon for me."

"You mean to tell me there ain't one of ya with the grit to ride with me?" Marshal Thorn asked, dumb-founded.

"You been sittin' around here for a year doin' pretty much nothin'," Ressie said. "It's high time you earned your keep, Billy Bob. We can't up and leave our busi-nesses. This here *is* your business."

"Don't you worry none, Marshal," Rap continued. "We'll take care of town while you're gone. Sheriff Hill ain't gonna be walking for another six months, if ever. One of them fellas in the James Gang winged him bad. I reckon it was just bad luck and a weak heart that killed the deputy. That bullet hole in his shoulder shouldn't have done him in him so quick."

Marshal Thorn chomped down on his quid and spat a yard of juice at Rap's feet before he turned and stormed off toward his office. He had to grab the wanted fliers on the James Gang, a couple of extra guns, and some trail supplies—pork, beans, and coffee. If he didn't linger, he might have a chance of finding their track.

Thorn was tough, a Kansas-born lawman with a no-nonsense character. There weren't many honest marshals so far west. Even though he had some ques-tionable shootings, he never stole a dime. That was more than he could say for about half the lawmen he knew. Then there were the sheriffs. Most educated towns knew better than to elect some fraud or fool. More often than not, the sheriff was elected for some-one's monetary or political gain. Marshals didn't get elected, and many stayed on the job until they died. Sheriffs, on the other hand, could lose their job from one election to another. They were politicians with a badge.

Sure, Marshal Thorn had killed a couple of men in questionable situations. One was unarmed, and the other was shot in the back. Since there were no eyewitnesses to the killings, it was a marshal's word over the families of the deceased. The way he saw it, both men were out to kill him. So, he would have been a fool to squander a chance to kill them first. Who was required to draw first was for dime novels and newspapers. In real life, you killed your opponent as quickly and safely as possible.

Killing an unarmed man mattered little to Thorn. The way he saw it, the outcome was all the better. Thorn knew as soon as a gun was drawn, the barrel would be pointing his way. Then again, half the lawmen west of the Missouri River were outlaws before they were lawmen. Some were even famous like Wyatt Earp and Wild Bill Hickok. Were they lawmen or were they guns for fire. Billy Bob figured a little of both.

He was content to be a marshal. That was the hand life dealt him, and he accepted it for what it was. What angered him was citizens like Ressie. He was right; it was Thorn's job to hunt down outlaws and not that of a bunch of men who hardly knew one end of a gun from the other. A posse improved the odds of success, though.

Thorn knew there were men in town who were good with weapons; some might have once been outlaws themselves. The James Gang had a lot of friends, too—even as far south as Texas.

He headed out anyway.

The sun baked the land, and cicadas filled the air with noise. Flies buzzed around Thorn's horse's head as it flicked its ears and swished its tail. The air smelled of saddle leather, horse, gun oil, and tobacco.

Thorn stopped near the entrance to the livery stable and took a long drag on his cheroot. He pulled off his hat and raked his hair out of his face with his fingers. He took one last puff, stubbed it out on the sole of his boot and looked around. The crowd vanished right after he asked for volunteers. Now, hardly a soul was on the street. The marshal squinted into the glare as he wheeled his horse toward the river.

He knew if he had any brains at all, he would be riding north and not chasing the most dangerous men in the country. He had resigned himself to his job long ago, though. He knew occasionally the job was difficult. It was just unlucky for him; he had to be chasing what was left of Bloody Bill Anderson's Marauders and William Quantrill's Raiders. More experienced men in killing couldn't be found in the country. Billy Bob knew he didn't have a chance, but he did his job anyway. It was all he knew. So, he carried on like he had for decades with his badge pinned over his heart.

CHAPTER 4

RUN FOR YOUR LIFE

THE JAMES GANG, INCLUDING JODI, JED, AND JOHN, RODE over the border, then wheeled their horses east along the Rio Grande River. This made it easy to run if the Mexican Federales showed up. They would have sufficient notice if the American lawmen decided to forget international boundaries and ford the river, too. It was just a little water anyway but enough to cover their tracks. Of course, they expected a posse to give chase, especially after the uproar in the courtroom. There was no way the judge would let this dog lay, not after being winged.

Jed and John had mixed feelings. Without Jesse, Jed never would have been able to break John out on his own. When Jesse shot the prosecuting attorney in the heart, everybody froze with fear. The gleam in his eyes was enough to make them feel someone had just walked over their graves. John and Jed had ridden and fought beside Jesse and Frank, so, his actions came as no surprise to them.

They were concerned that Jodi would get mixed up

in their old mess with the Raiders and the Marauders. That was a one bell they hoped wouldn't be rung. Jed and John were enlisted due to no decision of their own. But the vengeful killings by Jesse and Frank had an unhealthy passion. The older James brother's passion was fading with time. To his dismay, Jesse didn't share his views and believed the banks and railroads had to pay the damages from the Civil War inflicted on the South. They were all owned by rich Yankees, and he wanted to ruin them all. If he made a lot of money in the process, all the better. For Jesse James, there was nothing more pleasing than stealing large sums of Yankee money.

Who really knew what the James brothers thought would come out of all this? Frank sometimes talked of the future; Jesse hardly ever mentioned it. It was like he knew what it held and didn't believe it would be a lengthy wait. He seemed to know it would turn out badly in the end; there was no other way. Plus, Jesse showed no signs of accepting the loss of the war. He swore he would continue to fight on until he bankrupted the banks and railroad companies. They were his clear and present enemies. With no soldiers to fight, he made do with robbing the rich.

It was five hundred miles from El Paso to Eagles Pass, where Jesse and Frank wanted to cross back into the United States. They rode the whole way along the south bank of the Rio Grande, keeping to the old Comanche switchback trails and staying out of sight the best they could. It was hot, but they had plenty of water and good grazing. As Raiders, they were accustomed to riding for long days at neck-breaking speeds, especially when they were chasing enemies or running from their enemies.

At night they would take turns keeping watch from

high ground while the rest camped in an arroyo or a gully so they could make a small fire and have a hot meal and coffee. They were professionals at traveling fast. The hardship others experienced while riding hundreds of miles was their daily bread and butter. Even Jodi kept up to everyone's surprise. She proved to be an excellent rider and rarely tired.

On the fifteenth day, they camped south of Eagles Pass near Piedras Negras on the Mexican side of the river. They could have made it in ten days had they ridden east for Comstock, but even though it cost them another five days, it was much safer. They knew any posse would be made up of town citizens and, after a couple of weeks on the trail, they would long for their soft, city beds and all that went with a civilized life. Living on the trail might have felt adventuresome for most in the first days or maybe even a week. After two weeks, most would have abandoned the marshal's quest for justice.

Bob, Jim, John, and Coal rode together during the Civil War, but none of them could match Jesse's violence. He was their leader; it was evident to all. No one, not even Frank, challenged him or his authority. At times, Frank did question his judgment, though.

Jed and John didn't share a close bond with Jesse. They both knew what he was and considered him a friend, albeit dangerous to be around.

Tin spoons scraped metal pans as they finished their hot, salted pork and beans.

"What's the plan, Jesse?" Coal Younger asked. "I'm ready to hit town. Eagles Pass must have grown since the last time I was here."

Jed's eyes met John's, and they knew what each other

was thinking: *How were they going to get away from the James Gang without starting trouble or endangering Jodi.*

"I reckon we've left any posse that's after us a few days back now," Jesse said. "That's why I always say we need the best horseflesh we can find. It makes all the difference in the world."

When the riders forded the river and rode up the steep bank on the American side, they dismounted and waited to see if anybody spotted them. They hid the horses in dense brush and spread out to wait for the posse. They believed they had turned back by now, but only amateurs would take it for granted. They waited the entire day and late into the night. A posse never showed.

"What's the plan, Frank?" Bob Younger asked, "I'm gettin' tired of sleepin' on the ground."

"Would you rather be pushin' up roses from your grave?" John Washington asked.

"Nobody was talkin' to you, Black man," Bob snapped back. "I never did figure out you ridin' with the captain and all. I figure you must do black magic. I heard the slaves brought Voodoo from Africa's western coast to New Orleans. I heard tell you were from thereabouts. The newspaper called it 'New Orleans Voodoo.'"

"Don't talk nonsense," Frank said and laughed. "Don't forget, John fought alongside us all through the war. He was fighting with Captain Quantrill before the war broke out, weren't ya, John?"

John looked hard at Younger. There had always been friction between he and the Youngers because they still treated him like a slave. Bob resented his relationship with the captain. Maybe it was a mixture of pure racist hatred and envy. Quantrill didn't see any difference between his favorite scout and the others. In fact, sometimes he treated John better than the rest.

Dad gummed Jed Coal was just the same. He, too, treated John Washington like any other soldier. Bob didn't like it.

Bob Younger never thought about the countless times John snuck out into the night with Jed and killed threats before they could shoot any of them. He never considered the real reason why the captain liked the Black man so much.

At first, he thought he was the captain's personal slave. It was soon apparent that that was not the case because Quantrill truly considered John a friend. Apparently, he was more of a friend than Bob, an unforgivable fact. Younger didn't shed a tear when the captain was shot down by Union troops in Tennessee while trying to make it back home to Ohio.

Having the favored scout show up in his world again was nearly more than Bob could stomach. He thought he had been rid of him for good, but there he was. He never asked his brothers why they accepted him so easily. If Bob had his way, he would gun down John the first chance he got. If they knew what was good for them, John and Jed would best be on their way. If they stuck around, one of them could end up dead.

The sun dangled in the sky above the horizon like a puppet on a string. Glaring light stretched from the horizon and reached the other end of the earth. Finally, as it began to vanish, a rainbow of color blushed. Stars began to appear on the eastern edge of the world.

Jed, Jodi, and John had a moment alone for the first time in two days. The whole gang was spread out so nobody could catch them bunched up and make them easy targets.

"I hope you two don't intend to stay with Jesse and Frank," Jodi whispered. "You know Jesse is a time bomb waiting to go off at any minute. Plus, how would we divide what we rob from a bank nine ways? There'd be nothing left."

"You're forgetting Jesse saved my life back in El Paso," John said. "Without him and Frank, I would have hung back there."

"If we stay with Frank and Jesse, it may well be us who hangs," Jed said. "Jesse draws trouble like flies to manure."

"Why not just tell them we're leaving because we have plans," Jodi said. "We did intend to rob another bank, didn't we? I don't see us making any decisions that include the James Gang."

John shook his head. He frowned, spat in the dirt and said, "If'n y'all want you can go, but I've gotta stay to pay back my debt to Frank and Jesse."

"You know how Jesse is, John," Jed said. "He's mean to ya at times. All it takes is for him to go too far one day. He likes to let the lead fly. It's a miracle one of us ain't been shot. You saw how he shot up that courtroom."

"No, Jesse wouldn't shoot me," John said, shaking his head adamantly. "He'd never do that."

"The Youngers would, though," Jed said. "Especially Bob. You know as well as me, he don't like you or me. He don't think much of runnin' with a woman either."

"If'n you want, take Jodi and ride out," John said. "I'll be fine. I'm the one with the debt to repay." He gave them a sheepish smile and added, "You know there is honor among thieves."

Jed was shocked his partner would say such a thing. It was true he was involved with Jodi even though he never thought it would happen. He knew she was good for him, too. But John was like the only family he had had for years. They had been together through thick and thin. Each one had saved the other's life numerous times. There was no way Jed was ready to leave John to defend himself against the Youngers. Time would tell if Jesse kept defending him or not. Jessy's feelings often changed with the direction of the wind.

MARSHAL THORN HAD BEEN WORKING the job for a long time and was clever when tracking dangerous outlaws, especially when he was alone. After a week, he was sure where they were headed. Had he known for sure, he would have cut across the country rather than following the winding river. But he could have easily lost them, too, had they changed direction or headed north before Eagles Pass.

He believed the outlaws would head for somewhere with a bank they could rob. At least, that was what Thorn thought. And it wouldn't be in Eagles Pass. There wasn't enough money in that small bank to draw their interest. Instead, they probably would spend a day or two licking their wounds and resting from the hard ride. They would need money, and the James Gang only spent cash from banks or trains. Rather than cross the river at Eagles Pass, the marshal forded a half day before. Then, he circled wide of town before he entered. He wheeled his horse toward the Army fort nearby.

It would be much more discreet for him to tend to

his horse, eat, clean up and let some time pass before he looked at Eagles Pass. If he rushed things, he knew he would get himself killed. That is, if they came this way. He stayed clear of the river for half a day before the town to ensure he wasn't discovered.

The outlaws could have carried on toward Laredo, but that was another hard ride, and the horses would be worn out. He guessed the James Gang would be in town somewhere. Luckily for the marshal, the gang never saw his face. He unpinned the shiny star from his shirt and stuffed it into the pocket of his britches until he needed it. The badge was enough to get him killed if Jesse got a look at it. For the time being, he would be a rancher looking to purchase horses.

He suspected the outlaws might steal fresh horses before they lit out. It only stood to reason. If he knew where the best horses were available, he could get one step ahead of them.

Eagles Pass was a town with only a couple of places to sleep. One would be a fleabag dump, and the other crude but clean. The best place to wait would have been over the river in Pierdras Negras, but then he was too far away to see if they suddenly took off for who knows where.

Marshal Thorn sat against a tree with a view of the small town. His hat was pulled down low so he could just peek under the brim and hide his face in its shadow. He took a drag from his cigarette as he watched for movement. His face glowed orange. A frown creased his lips as he ran through the possibilities. He shook his head and muttered to himself when he caught the first glimmer of something he didn't like.

What if they split up? From the report back in El

Paso and the track he'd followed for two weeks, there were now nine of them. Once they re-entered the United States; it stood to reason they might break up into groups of two or three so they couldn't easily be recognized. So many heavily armed men stood out like a lamb in a trip of goats. They would probably split up here and regroup wherever the next bank or train robbery was planned.

Then, Billy Bob tried to think about what he would do when he finally came face-to-face with the gang. How in the world would he arrest or kill them without getting killed himself? That was something he still hadn't worked out. He just knew what he was supposed to do, and he planned to do it. He followed the murderers and hoped he could get them back to El Paso to stand trial, or old Judge Black would be an impossible headache.

CHAPTER 5

UNDER PRESSURE

JED COAL AND BOB YOUNGER HAD NEVER GOTTEN ALONG. It wasn't that they had an open argument or conflict. They simply just didn't like each other; they never did. Things in life changed, though; people do, too. Some of the changes lately rubbed Bob the wrong way. One of them was Jesse siding up with Jed after such a long absence. It was another reason he started treating John poorly. He had never figured out what a Black man was doing in Quantrill's Raiders. He knew better than to voice his opinion, though. The captain never let John stray too far from his side. William Quantrill always said he was the best scout he ever had.

Now, the two pop up all unexpected and poke their noses in the James Gang's business. There were enough of them to divide the spoils. Bob didn't see the need for more. Nobody messed with the James Gang anyway. Why did they need two of the old Raiders to do something they already did so well?

Plus, Jed had never been one of them. He wasn't even from Missouri. He was a regular soldier before he was forced to fight with the captain. Their old leader wasn't around to defend the Black man and the White fool. Not to mention bringing a woman into the gang. He knew there was no way for the new alliance to work out. It just wasn't the way he wanted things to be.

Of course, Bob realized Jed and John hadn't come looking for Frank and Jesse. It was all supposedly a big coincidence. He figured Jesse would turn on the Black man in time, but he knew the James brothers felt Jed was one of them, even if the Youngers didn't.

Bob felt Jed was not totally committed to the cause. Nobody could say he couldn't shoot or hadn't participated like the rest. There wasn't a man in the regiment with the body counts John and Jed had achieved. Jed was the best shooter he'd ever seen, and he'd seen a lot during the war. His kill numbers were unrivaled. He was as brave a man as any he knew. He just didn't like him because he ran with John Washington. That was it in a nutshell.

The room went quiet when the outlaws finally pushed their way into the Eagles Pass Saloon. It was a relatively small place but, then again, it was a small town. There was another one just like it across the street. They even had the same names. One said number one and the other number two and advertised beds for fifty cents a night.

A few hours later, John Washington walked out the door with Jed in tow. They gathered the reins of the horses and walked them toward the stables. Time had flown by as they ate and had a few sips of whiskey.

Jesse and Bob were loud as usual. The others tried to maintain some discretion. They didn't doubt the bartender thought they were outlaws. What else could they be? They arrive in a group, especially with a Black man armed to the teeth. The one who stood out like a dove among pigs was Jodi. With her blond hair, shapely figure and a pistol on her hip, she was a sight few men forgot easily. Just the combination of the outlaw gang was enough for everyone who saw them to remember, something Frank James disliked.

With Jed gone, Jesse couldn't help but flirt with his girl—he was just funning anyway.

"How did a pretty little thing like you get messed up with a quiet fella like Jed?" Jesse asked. "Why, I doubt you'd have as much fun with him as you would with me." He winked at her as he slipped out his revolver and twirled it on his finger, showing off in front of the attractive woman.

To Jesse's dismay, Jodi pulled her pistol and twirled it over and under her hand, finally flipping it into the air and grabbing the pistol grip before slipping it into the holster. The young outlaw's ears turned as red as tomatoes.

"I bet I can outshoot ya too, slick," Jodi said and snickered.

"Hold on, now," Frank James intervened. "We don't need to go makin' a bunch of noise. Let's just have a few drinks in peace without having a shootin' contest. I thought we were supposed to be discreet. How about you listen to me for once. Maybe we can spend a few days in town before we have to go on the run again."

"Discreet?" Jesse asked. "I'll show you discreet if ya want."

Right before he could pull his pistol, his brother grabbed him from behind in a bear hug and whispered in his ear.

"Simmer down, Jesse," Franks said. "We're on the run, boy. If you make a bunch of noise, we won't get to sleep in a soft bed tonight. And stop flirtin' with Jed's girl before she shoots ya. She looks to be on the ornery side to me."

Across the street, a man in a black hat walked out of the saloon and took a seat on the porch. Over the rim of his beer mug, he watched the other bar. He was waiting for something to happen. He walked to the edge of the building and sat his glass on the windowsill. Without even looking, he stepped into the alley, unbuttoned his britches, and relieved himself on the bushes. Nobody would ever take him for a lawman, even though he had a revolver strapped to his leg. Then again, pretty much everybody who lived in Texas was armed.

Marshal Thorn watched as a tall, thin man with distant eyes and a Black man gathered the horses' reins and headed toward the livery. In half an hour and a glass of whiskey later, they returned as the marshal sat in the shadows of the porch and watched every detail. He wasn't quite sure who the two men were, but he figured the Black man was from the El Paso courthouse the other was part of the James Gang.

He hoped to get a look at Jesse and Frank's faces to make sure it was them. The others must be the Youngers, but who could the Black man be? Logic told him he was the man on trial for murder. Since when did Negros ride with Rebel raiders, especially with the likes of Quantrill's soldiers? They were devils on horseback and as mean as they come. They were like no other group of Confederates sympathizers.

They disappeared inside, and a short time later, he heard a commotion. He fingered his walnut pistol grip as he strained his ears. Something was happening; the voices got louder as minutes passed.

Suddenly two men came busting through the saloon's batwing doors. They wrestled each other across the porch and out into the street. One of them was the tall fellow he saw with the Black man. The other he recognized from a wanted poster. It was Bob Younger.

~

WHEN JED WALKED into the saloon following John Washington, he immediately saw Jodi was as mad as the dickens. His eyes flashed toward Jesse, and he saw the smirk on his face and the anger in Frank's eyes.

"What's goin' on here?" Jed asked. "Whatcha been up to now, Jesse? You been messin' with my girl?"

"Oh, so she's your girl, now, is she?" Jesse sassed. "Don't get mad, Jed. I was just havin' some fun. I swear I didn't put a finger on her."

"I would have shot ya if ya had," Jodi spat. The venom in her voice surprised everybody, including Jesse and Jed. "I don't take to sass," she added and turned her attention to her glass.

Jed, like John were more fit than the others, but he had a particular natural calm posture about him. Like he knew something, the rest didn't. Maybe the vision of an experienced sniper made him that way. Or all of those soldiers he killed.

Bob Younger stepped forward with his known swagger and a lopsided grin. The potential hazard made them pause, as did his posture.

"I don't take kindly to you sassin' Jesse like that," Younger spat. "Do you think you can take me, too?"

"I couldn't say," Jed replied. "I've never tried."

If Jed was nervous, he didn't show it.

"I wasn't talkin' to you anyway. I was talkin' to Jesse," he added.

"Why are ya in such a hurry to get your butt kicked?" Bob spat. "If you sass Jesse, you sass me. We're the real members of the James Gang. Quantrill's dead and the war's over. You and Washington ain't one of us."

"Why are you startin' a fight with 'em, Bob?" Jesse asked. "It was me he was talkin' to, not you."

"I figured this's been a long time comin'. So, we might as well get it over with and out of our system," Bob said with a big grin.

"There's but one other possibility," Jesse said, taunting Bob.

"What's that?" Younger asked and flashed angry eyes.

"I know you don't talk much about your age, but you might be losing a step. Now, you wanna take on Jed to show us all you can still keep up."

Jesse laughed so hard his big belly rose and fell with each chuckle. Younger's face turned purple with anger. He couldn't hold it back any longer.

Jed and the rest of the gang tried to hide their amusement but couldn't. It just made Bob more furious. He lost his cool.

"Do you think this is funny?" Younger growled.

"No, sir. Absolutely not," Jed said with a smile.

Bob shuffled his feet as his face twisted into a scowl. Jed saw the punch coming from a mile away. Younger thought he was still fast, but he didn't even know what quick meant. Jed dodged and took a couple of feeble swings at the bully. He was taunting the outlaw, but Bob was too dumb to realize it.

Younger sensed more than he saw the left hook roaring toward his face. He tried to brace himself, pulling in his chin and dropping his hips. The bone-crushing blow landed on his left eye. His legs wobbled as he regained his balance. He had to shake his head to clear the fog. Then he was ready to go again.

Younger dropped into a crouch and moved slowly to his right. Jed began shifting left as he sought an angle of attack. He saw his opportunity when Bob faked a kick. Jed glimpsed an opening.

Younger decided to finish the quiet sniper then and there. He wasn't going to waste time dancing with him like a fool. He wanted him to feel some real pain. Maybe he could bust up his ribs and puncture a lung if he got lucky.

Anybody who did much fighting knew there were a load of punches from which to choose. There are haymakers, roundhouses, jabs, rabbit punches, hooks, and uppercuts. All four limbs and even your head were weapons.

Jed swung and hit Bob so squarely on the chin that it unhinged his jaw and knocked out four teeth. Younger blinked his eyes in disbelief right before his body dropped to his knees. He tried to keep his balance and not go down, but his effort was to no avail. In seconds he toppled over like a felled tree.

Jed believed he could size up an opponent in about twenty seconds. That was all it took for him to know if his opponent had enough talent to do you in. He knew in ten seconds Bob was going down. He also knew he would get up.

"I'm gonna make you feel pain like you've never

thought possible," Jed said in just over a whisper as Bob shook the cobwebs from his brain.

Younger pushed himself off the floor and came at Jed again. It wasn't with the same confidence he did on the first pass. He rushed forward on pure anger and adrenaline. Jed could smell tobacco and coffee on his breath. When he hit Bob in the throat, he howled and grabbed at his neck.

"I told you not to bite off more than you could chew," Jesse said, pointing a finger in Bob's face.

Jed looked at Jodi to see if she was all right. He cracked a smile in an attempt to brush off the incident. He stepped up to the porch and cleared his throat. He stood before her as she inched closer.

Jed squared his shoulders and asked in a tight voice, "Are you all right, darlin'?"

Jesse laughed like he was having a great time. He got bored quickly and was always eager for any kind of action.

"Great outlaws don't complain about the rules." Jesse chuckled. "They just find ways around 'em."

CHAPTER 6

FRIENDLY DEPARTURES

ONCE JIM, JOHN, AND COLE YOUNGER CARRIED BOB OUT of the street and back into the saloon, a crowd began to form. Even though it was a small town, when anything happened interesting, the bored citizens came rushing to gawk. Jesse was oblivious to the danger. He liked the attention. He laughed and cackled like a hen. Nobody was having more fun than Jesse James.

Bob had a broken jaw and a damaged eye. Time would tell if he would see out of it again. The beating took the wind out of his sails and rendered him harmless. Cole found it funny, but Jim and John were embarrassed. Everybody was edgy—except for Jesse, and he didn't appear to give a danged about what anybody thought or said. After fifteen days of hard riding and boredom, he was having a grand time.

Across the street sat a man in the black hat. He watched the spectacle and didn't know what to make of it. Bob Younger sure did get himself a beating. He wondered who the tall fellow with the thousand-yard stare was. He never saw him on a James Gang wanted poster. Then he remembered the Black man who was nowhere to be seen. The blonde-haired woman stood with her hip cocked and fist perched on her gun.

He could see Jesse James standing in the middle of the fracas. He was the only one laughing. Behind him stood Frank James. He was staring at his brother with angry eyes. He clearly disapproved of his brother's actions. It drew attention to the gang but didn't appear to concern the young outlaw. He seemed to welcomed action—especially if it was violent.

Suddenly the young outlaw looked at the man sitting on the porch across the street. It was as though he had some sixth sense and felt him watching. His gaze was like that of a wild animal looking for prey. He knew he was the king of his jungle and feared no one.

Billy Bob Thorn felt his butt pucker, and hackles stood on his neck as goose bumps sprouted on his arms. He felt death cast its shadow over his soul. He wondered what he was doing. He sat there and waited until, finally, Jesse looked away.

Marshal Thorn sighed deeply, the sound of relief one makes when nearly missing death. Jesse was occupied elsewhere. He knew there was no way to approach such a gang. He would have to continue to follow to see if he couldn't catch at least one of them — maybe even Jesse James — alone. Or follow them to a town big enough to have a sheriff and deputies to assist. Maybe they could surprise them on their next bank job. There were a lot of *ifs* in Thorn's formula, but it was the only two chances he had.

The other way was to go at them head-on. Sure, he may kill one of them, but he'd probably be shot dead before he cleared leather. The only way was to bushwack them and even an ambush was sketchy. Many men had tried during the war and failed. It was said Quantrill and Anderson often charged into battle fighting three- or four-to-one odds. The difference was his men were experts with years of experience. The average lawman pulled his gun a few times in anger at the most.

As soon as the young outlaw turned away, Billy Bob jumped off the porch and hid in the bushes in the alley. From there, he could still see the front of the saloon, but they couldn't see him. When he looked down, he saw he was standing in a puddle of liquid and cursed.

WHEN BOB YOUNGER was carried into the saloon, he was out cold. They lay him out on a couple of tables pushed together and called for a doctor to tend to his injuries. His jaw seemed to be unhinged and was hanging to one side. Jesse looked at the unconscious man and harrumphed.

"You got what ya asked for, Bob," Jesse said and laughed. "I told ya you ain't as quick as you was at nineteen. You're ain't a teenager anymore, boy. If you keep sittin' around in saloons, you'll soon be gettin' soft. You can see for yourself; John and Jed are in shape and as hard as nails. Most times you run out of breath headin' for the outhouse."

Bob was too battered to sass back. Soon, Dr. Adams walked through the doors and everybody's eyes turned his way. The doctor squinted at the men with suspicion. He saw all the guns, clicked his tongue, and shook his head.

"All right, where's the injured man?" the doctor asked.

Bob had one hand holding his jaw closed. Every time he let go, one side dropped an inch.

"Move your hand so I can see whatcha got," the doctor said as he had a look. "That's as broken as an outhouse door. I'll have to wire it shut. I'm afraid you'll have to drink your food for a few weeks."

"It won't stop him from talkin', will it, Doc?" Jesse asked, feigning concern.

"I'm afraid it will," Adams replied as he studied the damage. "He lost a few teeth and all. What happened? Did a mule kick 'em?"

"Why old Jed here has done solved our problem then." Jesse laughed. "Bob won't be flappin' his jaw for a spell, and we'll be left in peace. How do you like then chickens, John Washington?"

The fact Jesse just carelessly gave the doctor and every onlooker John's full name and identified Bob and Jed didn't go unnoticed by the old sniper team. Now, they were probably going to be mixed up with the James Gang, which was precisely what they were trying to avoid.

"I don't take to being someplace I ain't wanted," Jed said. "I reckon John, the girl and me best be on our way."

"So, now I'm the girl, am I?" Jodi sassed back. "Maybe I'll just leave on my own. I don't need you two either."

Washington stepped to the cowgirl's side and whispered, "Quiet down a bit before everybody in town knows who we are, especially since you ain't been named yet. It was for your own good. These walls have ears."

"Whatcha say, Jesse?" Washington turned and asked. "Will ya hold it against me for leaving after you saved my bacon and all?"

"Aw, shucks, John," Jesse said. "You know you'll

always be one of us. Go on. If'n Jed stays; he might just kill Bob if he has a go at him again. Bob sure is stupid enough to try."

He laughed loud and hard. Lucky for them all, the youngest James brother was in a good mood. Not even one of the Youngers would stand up to Jesse. Everybody in the room knew how fast he was and with what ease he killed. They had seen how quickly he could change from cheerful and happy to mean, ornery, and full of blood-lust. It was best to let things lay where they fell.

Jesse and Frank wanted John in the gang to track and Jed for his sharpshooting skills. Bob saw to it that wasn't going to happen, though. Maybe they should have gotten rid of Bob. It was too late now. Cole Younger wouldn't stand for it anyway.

The Black man, the fighter and a blonde woman walked out of the saloon only to return a half hour later with their horses and towing a mule packed with provisions. Marshal Thorn got a good look at the horses—two grays and a roan. He knew these horses would be changed for fresh ones as soon as they traveled for a few days. He backed down the alley to ensure Jesse didn't see him again and decided to investigate. He had to wait until they all left. Soon they would be drunk and ready to sleep off the whiskey and the hard, two-week ride. All Marshal Thorn had to do was sit tight.

As soon as he had more information, he would follow the two men and the woman. He couldn't remember them on any wanted posters, but now he had a name. John Washington and Jed something. It wasn't as much as he would like, but it was a start.

Thorn thought the best way to go about it was to pick off the weakest members of the gang first. How dangerous could a woman be? The Black man looked to be aging, and he already knew how fast the tall one was. He'd seen him tear Bob Younger to pieces—like he was chopping wood. They called him Jed, and he would be the one to give him a problem if there was one.

Billy Bob believed if he waited long enough, the answers would come to him, and an opening would appear. Maybe he could steal the girl and hold her for ransom. One way or another, he had to work out a plan that allowed him to ride back to El Paso alive—hopefully with one or two members of the James Gang.

"NEXT TIME you ignore me like you did, I might just shoot you, Jed Coal," Jodi warned. She was as angry as they had ever seen her.

"It was the shock of seeing Jesse and Frank sittin' there, knowing somethin' had happened to John," Jed replied.

"When you had something to be jealous about, you were aware enough of me, now weren't ya?" Jodi retorted.

"If I were you two, I'd focus on getting as far from town as we possibly can and quick. There was too much talkin' back there with Jesse and the boys. He called me by name and you too, Jed. There'll be folks that remember what was said. Just you watch. That's why I stepped in. Jesse was just about to mention your name, too. Then you really would be considered one of us. So far, you might be able to talk your way out of trouble if they catch us. That is if'n they don't shoot us first."

The three of them rode north toward San Antonio.

They sometimes found the best way to get lost was in the biggest crowd they could find.

"Are you sure you want to go back to San Antonio after we robbed the bank on the square?" John asked.

"They didn't get a look at us," Jodi said. "The city is so big we easily can get lost in a different part of the town. All we have to do is wait until the James Gang robs another bank. Anyone who might be watching us or on our tail will follow them and not us."

As they traveled north as fast as the horses permitted, John felt like somebody was following them. The feeling was contagious; all three of them soon looked over their shoulders. As the days passed, a full moon appeared. They stopped traveling during the day and traveled at night instead. They would ride until they were worn out and the horses near collapse. The slept for four hours and were back on the trail north with John carefully leading the way. Nobody was taking any chances since the gunfight at the courthouse in El Paso. They had ridden in a big circle and were finally coming to the end of the hundred-forty-mile ride. Just like when John and Jed were in the Raiders, they traveled long distances in a short time.

They left the switchback trails and wheeled their horses onto the main road when they were a few miles away. Wagons, horses, carts and people became denser as they neared the city. Soon they were enveloped in the masses and quickly lost themselves, dodging down alleys and using backstreets to make sure no one was following.

After two hours of cat and mouse, John believed they had shaken whoever he felt was on their tail. They checked into a modest hotel and led their horses to the smallest livery they could find.

Washington immediately broke off from Jed and Jodi and began to backtrack. He wanted to know who was trailing them. Identifying your enemy was essential before you let your guard down.

Jed and Jodi got a suite at the hotel and didn't leave their room for three days. Especially after John came back with the bad news his gut feeling was right. There was a lawman following them. They had shaken him, but he wasn't giving up; he had followed them from El Paso.

They decided to batten down the hatches and wait it out. John knew where the marshal was staying but he didn't know where they were. He would scour all the saloons where outlaws hung out, but he wouldn't find them.

CHAPTER 7

THE JAMES GANG

"COME ON, FRANK," JESSE SAID. "WE'VE BEEN HERE TOO long, and you know it. I say it's time to rob a bank. We can make a beeline for San Antonio. It's less than a hundred fifty miles. We could do what Jed and John did and rob two banks at once."

"Is robbing banks all you ever think about?" Frank asked.

"Yep, that and trains. I intend to rob banks until the rich Yankee owners back East suffer," Jesse spat. "If'n ya wanna hurt a wealthy Northerner, you gotta get 'em where it hurts the most—in his pocketbook."

By the time the James Gang hit San Antonio, John, Jed, and Jodi had been hiding out in their hotel room for several days. They had no clear idea where the James brothers would go after Eagles Pass, but San Antonio was on the way to pretty much everywhere. They were sure they wouldn't head for Mexico again. So, even if they didn't hit a bank there, they figured they would probably pass through just the same. Hopefully, the marshal tailing them would get wind of the James Gang.

As loud as Jesse was, there was always a chance he would let it be known he was around.

Unless they decided to rob another bank in town, they would lay low until the day of the James heist. Jesse was rowdy, but he wasn't stupid. He always had Frank to keep watch over him if he decided to make a rash decision or do something that jeopardized their freedom.

"Let's go get some of that chili they sell on the square," Jesse said. "I'm so hungry I could eat a dog."

"If'n, you're not careful which stand you eat at; you may well be eatin' dog," Bob Younger mumbled.

With his jaw wired shut, he was hard to understand. The good part was he spoke less than usual. The rest of the gang poked fun at him like he was always poking fun at them. With the tables now turned, he didn't like it one bit.

"Now, ya get a little dose of whatcha give out, Bob," Jesse said and laughed. "You're always hackin' on somebody. Now, maybe you'll mind your manners when you're outmatched."

"I wasn't outmatched," Bob mumbled. "He tricked me is all."

"He tricked you with a fist the size of a horse apple is what he did," Frank added. He, too, laughed. "He left your eye starin' off somewhere the other eye ain't."

"You'd have thought he would have knocked some sense into you, but it appears not," Cole Younger said.

"I should have taught ya how to kill 'em," Jesse bragged. "That's as simple as pie. You point the weapon, pull the trigger and bam. A chuck of lead enters your target, bustin' up vital organs and it's all she wrote. If'n you're brave enough; you can sneak up on 'em and slip a knife through his armpit and pop his heart like a bloated body, too. I can show you a hundred ways to stamp your ticket. The way you look, I believe you need some learning."

To Bob's dismay, the whole gang—his brothers included—laughed at him. It was high time they got even with his ornery disposition and poor manners. The more they laughed, the angrier he got, though. He was the whipping boy all the way to San Antonio. When the James Gang got into town, they stayed in the Menger Hotel, one of the newest in town. It was only built in 1865, and offered fine dining and a well-stocked bar. It had a grand porch out front with dozens of wicker chairs.

It was expensive, so only the rich and affluent frequented the establishment. It just happened to be one of the hotels Marshal Thorn walked by daily. He knew the gang had money. After riding from El Paso to Eagles Pass and finally on to San Antonio, he knew the gang would be looking for luxury. Most successful bank robbers had plenty of money to spend on themselves. Jesse and Frank weren't the modern-day Robin Hoods they sometimes were made out to be in the Southern newspapers. They never gave a dime to anybody that wasn't in the gang. After their stint in the Civil War most of them had forgotten what Southern manners were.

Once the James Gang checked into the hotel, they paid a boy to take their horses to be brushed down and fed. They headed for the square and some of the best food in the city. The Chili Queens served it on Military Plaza. Dozens of stands boasted the best *chili con carne* in the United States and Mexico. Many people had the misconception Mexicans invented chili, but it dated back to the Spanish as a meat and bean stew.

There were long tables scattered about the plaza. All types of men and women from different levels of society ate side by side. Bankers ate beside paupers. Fancy-dressed women enjoyed their meal across from ladies of the night. The square was one of the few places social classes and standing had little place. The six gang members sat on a long bench that ran the length of the large kitchen table. Twenty people sat shoveling the delicious dish into their mouths. Hardly a word was sad as they all enjoyed the delicacy.

MARSHAL THORN HAD BEEN WAITING at Military Plaza every day from just before noon. Each day he picked a different table to enjoy his meal so he wouldn't get friendly with any of the servers. It was better nobody noticed him. That was why he continued to spy without his badge on his chest. He looked like any one of the hundreds of people who came to eat dinner daily. Most people put up a guard as soon as they saw a badge. Many lawmen this far west were as hard as nails; some had been outlaws themselves in other state. Until now, he had seen no sign of the three outlaws he followed from Eagles Pass.

He still couldn't figure out what a Black man was doing with the likes of Quantrill's Raiders, whose entire mission was to maintain states' rights and block abolition. The marshal believed it was only a matter of time before the main part of the gang caught up with the rest of the outlaws. If he was lucky, he could catch them casing a bank. Then Thorn could inform local authorities and obtain solid backup for when things got serious.

He knew the James Gang would never surrender to the law of their own will. Undoubtedly, they would put up a fight. They hadn't stopped fighting since the end of the Civil War. A shootout with marshals wasn't something they would shy away from.

After a week of sitting at different tables and consuming large quantities of chili, Thorn finally got sight of Jesse and Frank James. They arrived with the four Younger brothers and walked around like they owned the place.

Cole, Jim, John, and Bob Younger followed Jesse and Frank, standing against a building with a solid wall at their backs. He could tell how they casually looked around for danger. The only one that didn't appear to worry about anything was Jesse. He seemed to have a good time wherever he went.

Thorn felt he had just hit the jackpot. All he had to do was follow the gang back to their hotel. Once he knew where they stayed, he could contact the closest lawmen. The James Gang was wanted all over the country. So, he believed the local marshals or sheriffs would be just as interested as him in these outlaws. Whoever caught the James Gang would go down in history. He planned to let all the credit go to the locals.

Marshal Thorn wasn't a man to brag or boast. He'd rather stay out of the limelight. For a man in his profession, it was dangerous to become famous. Some outlaw just might view him as a challenge and come gunning for him. No, it wasn't wise to be a renowned marshal or sheriff. Fame was one of those things that could turn out killing a man like him, and he had no interest in seeing his name in print—especially in the obituaries. All Thorn wanted to do was his job.

He was on his third bowl of chili when the James Gang finished and headed for the other side of the plaza. Billy Bob dropped four bits on the table and walked off the plaza before discreetly checking his gun. It wouldn't do to have an unloaded or jammed weapon if they suddenly turned on him. None of the gang seemed to care if someone was following them, but he knew they were being cautious. It just didn't look like it. There it was again. Frank James glanced around every few minutes.

The marshal was walking down the boardwalk on the opposite side of the street when he saw them stop and take in the buildings around them. Thorn quickly turned and looked into a shop window. It was a tool store, and he acted like he was window shopping when he was using the reflection of the glass to spy on the outlaws across the street.

Finally, they entered the fancy Menger Hotel. Now, he believed he had them. He would stick around for a while and make sure they didn't go back out. They might have popped in for a drink and intended to go somewhere else.

When a lawman stalked men like the James Gang, he had to ensure he had all his ducks in a row. Tanking unnecessary chances weren't in the criteria.

If Thorn went to the local law and was mistaken about where they lodged, it could cost him his reputation. If they all made mistakes, it would cost lives.

CHAPTER 8

PAYING DEBTS

JOHN WASHINGTON LEFT HIS FANCY CITY CLOTHING WITH his kit so he looked like any other poor Black man who was struggling to get by in San Antonio, Texas. He found a destitute man in an alley and purchased his clothing. He traded them for enough money to eat for a month. The only Black man to ride with Quantrill's Raiders now looked like most of the Negros after the war. Sure, the slaves were freed, but their lives hadn't changed as much as they wished, needed, or hoped.

Washington had been infiltrating the enemies' lines for years. This wasn't really all that different. He was a wealthy outlaw, acting like a poor freedman on the outs. When people passed, he tipped his hat but kept his eyes on the ground. That would be what the Southerners expected, and it assured nobody would remember his face. He shuffled along until he saw the lawman freeze and turn his head to the large glass window of a store. He was using it like a mirror.

John had to stifle a chuckle. He knew he was watching the man who was spying on the James Gang.

He had to admit he was pretty good at tailing—at least in a city. John had circled around enough times to know somebody had followed them all the way from El Paso. This was the man. He wasn't a Texas Ranger because he didn't wear a beige hat. He figured him for a US Marshal, the kind of man to chase down men like Jesse and Frank James. Sheriffs rarely ventured out of their counties, but marshals were required to go where and when needed.

"For a lone marshal to hunt down the James Gang, he's gotta have a death wish," John whispered to himself.

He assumed Jesse and Frank were somewhere in town unless they passed San Antonio entirely and headed for safer country. Of course, San Antonio was one of the best places to hide out in plain sight. At least if you were discrete about it, like Jed, Jodi, and John. For the James Gang, it might not work out that way because of Jesse's wild ways. If it weren't for Frank, he would have been shot and killed long ago.

That didn't mean he was a daisy. He could draw faster than most men and was more than willing to kill; sometimes he was eager. That was what made him so dangerous. Most men hesitate before they take a life; not the James brothers. They had lived through the Centralia Massacre. It was the bloodiest battle in all of the Civil War. John and Jed were there too. They both bore the same scars Jesse did. It was a bloodbath, and nobody escaped the phycological effects.

John understood he was in the James brothers' debt. If it weren't for Jesse standing up and shooting that prosecutor in El Paso and breaking him out, he would be hung and buried by now. He knew all too well that this was a debt that was to be repaid. The sooner he evened the score, the better for everybody. He wanted to stay as far away from the James Gang as possible, just like Jed and especially Jodi. When she was alone in the same room as Jesse, she was afraid but refused to admit it. There was something raw about the young man that scared her to the very core.

John knew he had to make the debt right before he abandoned his old friends. They rode together for four years; they knew each other like brothers, maybe even better than most brothers. None of them were the same after Centralia. They never talked about it, but it was burned into their memories forever. There was nothing they could do to get rid of the nightmares of that dreadful night.

When the James Gang entered the Menger Hotel, the marshal turned and waited for them to disappear. Then, he casually strolled across the street. He even had the cojones to have a seat on the porch. John picked up the box he had bought at the general store and shuffled across the street, his heels leaving a small wake of dust.

He walked up to the first man on the hotel porch and asked, "Y'all want a shoeshine? Best shine in San Antonio."

Without even looking at John, the man put his foot on the wooden box as he opened a new tin of shoe polish and began to rub it in with his fingers. The marshal was doing his best to look at the hotel's interior without appearing suspicious. The Black man busied himself with the fancy boots. When he was done, the man handed him two bits without a single word. It was as if John wasn't there; they treated him like he was a piece of furniture, not a man. He moved to the next man, but was ignored and brushed away.

Then he stood before the marshal and said, "Them's

some might dusty boots ya got on there, mister. How about I clean 'em up for ya?"

Just like the first man with fancy boots, the marshal set his foot on the box and strained to look through the large picture window in the front of the hotel.

"Do you want 'em normal brown or dark brown, sir?" John asked. "It's kind of hard to tell which one they was when they was new."

The marshal took a moment to look at the Black man at his feet.

"Anything brown will do," Thorn replied. "Put plenty of polish on 'em, so the leather don't dry out. It'll be a spell before I get a chance to tend to my boots again."

"Yes-sir." John smiled. "When I'm done, they'll be like brand new."

When the shoeshine was done, Thorn did just like the last man. He dropped two bits into the palm of John's hand without even looking him in the eye. John debated on killing him right there. He had his long, thin, skinning knife hidden. Cutting the artery on the inner part of his thigh would be simple. He would bleed out in minutes. He would draw attention to the hotel, though. He decided he would have to kill him in some other way, not where Frank and Jesse were staying. It would bring on the heat immediately, even though it was a perfect opportunity. He knew he could get away before anyone noticed the marshal was bleeding to death. All it would take would be a flick of his skilled wrist. He had killed several men that way.

Instead, he moved to the next man on the porch and began to shine his shoes. He kept watching the marshal out of the corner of his eye, though. John must have shined every boot on the porch, and still, the marshal sat.

He didn't even have a drink. He was consumed by his mission. He was on the brink of tackling the James Gang, and this was his only chance to get them all at once and not get killed in the process.

When Marshal Thorn finally stood, he stretched his back with his hands on his hips. Washington had moved to the other side of the street in the shadows of an alley. He had a perfect view of the entire front of the hotel. He searched the second-floor windows, looking for signs of any of the James Gang. Lucky for them, it appeared they didn't have rooms facing the street, or Jesse would be perched up there, curious about what was happening in the bustling city.

When the marshal finally stepped from the porch, he looked both ways as though he was uncertain where he was going. That was when it dawned on John; he was looking for the nearest sheriff or marshal's office. If he could get the cavalry together in time, they could box in the James Gang. There would be no way for them to escape. John had to tell Frank right immediately, so they had time to get out of the hotel.

He dropped his shoeshine box and roared across the street but was stopped at the doors. He was forbidden entry before he got a foot inside. A large doorman stood in his way. He wasn't about to allow a poor Black man inside. Suddenly, it dawned on him. He wasn't dressed in his fancy duds. To the hotel staff, he was just another poor person. There was no way he would get into the hotel like he was dressed. Was there time to change clothes? He was sure there would be a law office somewhere close. If he remembered right, it was in a large building named the Bat Cave. It housed the local law— both sheriff and marshal.

He looked up and down the street, but nothing came to mind. Finally, he pulled his guns and decided to force his way into the hotel. He had to warn Frank and Jesse, no matter what the risks. He owed them, and he always honored a debt.

Two women sat on a porch glider sipping coffee when John suddenly appeared. He looked like a street bum with a brace of cannon in his fists as he followed the barrels into the hotel. The first woman screamed; so did the second. John shot out the picture window sending all the people in the reception and bar diving for the floor. Half the people on the porch ran for their lives. Curiosity won over the other half. John sent two well-placed shots into the wall next to the bartender's head, and he stopped reaching for the scattergun under the bar.

Bullets flew through the air with apparent abandon, but John knew where every shot hit. He intended to frighten and not kill anybody if it was possible. He had never killed civilians unless he rode with Bloody Bill. Then, there didn't appear to be any rules. All that was in the past, though. Capt. Anderson was long dead.

John and Jed never liked killing civilians. They would shoot and kill an enemy and never think about it twice. Citizens were off limits, as were needless killings. Jed Coal felt the same way. Since Jed and he went on the run, they had only shot those who tried to shoot them. Hopefully, he wouldn't have to kill anyone now.

Of course, the gunfire brought Jesse and Frank storming down the stairs like racehorses. As soon as they saw the shooter was John Washington, they knew something was amiss. Jesse pulled his pistols and fired rounds at the front door, making the curious spectators duck for cover.

Two men came from a back room with guns in their fists. Jesse saw them halfway down the stairs and put a bullet into each heart. They fell to the floor like sacks of grain. His eyes searched the room for more threats.

Jesse ran up to John and asked, "What the hell's goin' on?"

"A marshal's got the hotel staked out and is headed for reinforcements. You boys got to get out of here and quick."

"How did you know?" Frank asked.

"I felt somebody followin' us for days now. So, I thought I'd have a look around. I found some marshal tailing us both. He followed you boys from Military Plaza and to the hotel so he could call for help. I figure we've got minutes before he shows up with a posse. The folks of San Antonio won't be as reluctant as the people back in Eagles Pass."

"Is he wearin' a black hat?" Jesse asked, suddenly remembering the man on the porch on the border.

"Yep," John replied.

"I seen that fool back in Eagles Pass," Jesse said. "He was sittin' on the porch of the saloon across from us. I noticed him because I felt his eyes on me. Something must have distracted me, or I'd have checked 'em out," Jesse said. "I owe you one, John."

"Nope, we're even, Jesse," John replied." You saved me back at the hearing with that crazy judge."

"I should have killed the lawman with the black hat when I had the chance down south," Jesse said.

By then, Frank was beside them both, nodding his

head. "We're even then, John. Until the next time, of course." He looked at his brother and raised an eyebrow.

"I know. I know," he said, robbing him of his last word. "It's time to go."

Frank turned around and climbed the stairs two at a time, with Jesse following. They sprinted for the Younger brothers to warn them of the danger. They would all flee out the back. The jig was up in San Antonio, and it was time to get out of town.

The people in San Antonio had more sand than the little village of Eagles Pass. Here men would be looking to make a reputation. Killing Jesse and Frank James would be the best trophy a gunfighter could acquire.

John made sure the James Gang made their getaway before the law arrived. Then, he vanished down an alley and into the masses of the large city. To anyone watching, he was just another Black man living on the street. His guns were hidden in a canvas sack he carried at his side. He made a beeline for the hotel with Jed and Jodi. It was time for them to leave, too.

When he returned to the hotel, they nearly didn't let him in there either. Finally, he proved he was registered and had a room, and they finally let him in. It was lucky for them because he was ready to pull iron and go in blazing. He ran up the stairs and hammered on the locked door.

"Who is it?" Jodi asked.

"It's me, John. Get this door open, girl. We got trouble."

She pushed the door open a crack, let John slip by, and then looked up and down the hall. She had her six-shooter in her fist and her eyes followed the barrel.

Nobody was there, so she slammed the door and turned the lock.

John quickly cleaned up, put on some riding clothes, and grabbed his carbine rifle. Jed already had his ear to the door, ready to open it and fire if the posse showed before they could get away.

Jodi grabbed her things and stuffed them into her saddlebags before they all climbed out the window. They crept across the roof to the back of the hotel and shimmed down a drainpipe to safety. In minutes, they were lost in the crowd, just like the James Gang.

Although hunted, they could hide in plain sight in the city but had to decide what to do next. They doubted the marshal would give up if he followed them this far. No, he would go all the way. There was no turning back for him. He was far too invested in capturing the James Gang.

When Marshal Thorn finally showed up at the hotel with a dozen armed deputies, he found a shot-up saloon and a bunch of terrified people. Jesse and Frank James had just filled the place full of holes. Two men were dead. The lawmen Thorn managed to round up all knew they were on the trail of the most wanted men in the United States.

"Who wants to form a posse?" Marshal Thorn asked.

Suddenly he was surrounded by men who wanted to sign up. Half of them looked like gunslingers; the rest were the marshals and deputies he brought to the hotel with him. Finally, he had his posse.

None of the volunteers were weak of heart, and all of them had killed. The posse consisted of two marshals, several deputies, a sheriff and even two bounty hunters

who happened to be at the sheriff's office when Thorn
went in to sound the alarm.

CHAPTER 9

BILLY BOB THORN

WHEN MARSHAL THORN ARRIVED AT THE MENGER Hotel, the blood drained from his face. Even though he had rushed as quickly as he could, the James Gang had somehow discovered they were on the way and fled. He could see the glass and splintered wood from gunfire. He talked to the witnesses, who all confirmed the presence of a crazy Black man who had been shining shoes not an hour before the ruckus.

When he returned, he arrived with a brace of pistols and apparently shot the place up. Nobody knew who the shoeshine man was, but they easily identified Frank James with his brother, Jesse.

Thorn knew the Black shoeshine man had to be the outlaw they planned to hang for murder back in El Paso. He should have recognized him when he was shining his shoes. He had him within his grasp and didn't even bother to consider who he was. Was he slipping with age? He had been tricked like a beginner. The shoeshine man was partnered with the man and woman he had followed for days.

They had led him to a payload—the James and Younger brothers. All were wanted for murder, robbery, and extortion. As far as he could tell, the Black man probably wasn't who the judge thought he was either. Most likely, Axel Black had believed he was just another freed slave. This man was no slave, though. He was just as much a killer and as dangerous as the James brothers.

Billy Bob knew he had to be more careful. They knew the law was on their trail, making things more dangerous every step of the way. Hopefully, they would split up again, so he and his posse could finally get a chance to have a go at them.

They met in front of the bullet-riddled hotel an hour later. Horses hooved hammered the street as dust billowed in their wake. They rode holus-bolus north to look and see if they could find the outlaws' tracks. The marshal knew they were running their horses too hard and should take a more cautious approach. If they baked the animals, they could be set afoot and easily picked off one at a time. If they rushed too much, they could ride directly into a trap and be killed.

But with the prey so close, they all felt the need to hurry and threw caution to the wind. Riding with so many big city marshals and sheriffs, he would never be allowed to call the shots.

San Antonio's Bat Cave Marshal, Hard Talk, took the lead. When he said jump, everybody in the building got nervous. He was a man of few words and only knew one speed—full out. He believed they would find the James Gang's trail, sneak up on them at night and engage in a turkey shoot. Marshal Talk already stated he intended to take no prisoners.

They were pretty sure they wouldn't go to Austin,

although it was another sizable city. Marshall Talk found the James Gang's trail at the end of the second day. He had been a tracker and hunter for the Army in his youth.

They pressed their horses even harder and looked for ranches where they could commandeer new mounts. They found only horses unfit for such a race. They would have to back off some and stick with the animals they had.

"I only count six riders," Marshal Thorn said.

"Jesse's with 'em," Hard Talk said. "I can feel it in my bones."

"That means there's still the two other fellas—the White Rebel and the Black man," Thorn explained. "I doubt the woman with 'em will be a problem, but the Black fella is. He's why the James Gang got away in San Antonio and the fella who shot up the hotel."

"If'n, you're afraid you can head on back to El Paso," Hard Take spat. "We can take care of this bunch of pups."

Billy Bob simmered but held his tongue. It irked him Marshal Talk was so quick to send him home after he had done all the hard work. He would probably try to claim all the credit, not alone the bounty money if they caught them.

Thorn wasn't as confident as Marshal Talk. He had seen how easily the outlaws slipped away from him for weeks. He doubted they would be easy to catch up with and pin down, especially if the other two were out there watching their backs.

The tracks led them toward Fredericksburg, where a large German settlement thrived. The outlaws probably would procure new horses and provisions there. They had no time to secure supplies, because they fled San

Antonio so suddenly, Thorn suspected. If they took too long to catch up, they would have fresh horses and all the supplies they needed to head for Kansas or Missouri.

That was where they suspected Jesse and Frank would go. Somewhere they had plenty of sympathizers and could hold up in some distant cabin until the heat passed. They had done the same thing time and again. Jesse just couldn't stay away from Clay County. It was his home, and the reason Jesse fought so hard, so claimed his brother.

Billy Bob believed Jesse had lost sight of his objective. The young man started fighting in the war at the early age of sixteen. Quantrill thought he was too young to join up with him and his brother Frank. So, he went for the next most notorious band of fighters—Bloody Bill Anderson and his Marauders. There wasn't a bloodier group of men in all the South, and it was where the James brothers learned to escape pursuit. Over and over again they seemed to get away.

When they were caught in a trap and forced to fight, their years of experience showed in how they battled. They were tenacious and not afraid to die, unlike most lawmen and bounty hunters who hunted them. All of the gang were crack shots, but the brains were with Frank and Jesse. Cole Younger struck Thorn as an intelligent man, but his brothers' reputations didn't impress him. Nonetheless, they knew how to kill. If not for their skills, they would be dead by now, being every lawman in the country was looking for them.

WHEN THE POSSE stormed into Fredericksburg, they got the attention of everyone. The men spread out with weapons drawn as they raced their horses up and down the main street. Women dropped their packages and ran for cover. Men ducked behind walls and pulled their guns. When the dust settled, the defenders finally saw the sunlight flash off all the tin stars.

The locals still didn't drop their guard. They knew half the lawmen in Texas had troubled pasts. Most men who took to the gun already had some experience. Then, there were the men left over from the war. Men from both sides rode south to Texas, but most were Confederates. The war was long over, but a few wild men still tried to carry on the struggle. Was it for politics, or was it for greed? The latter seemed to be the main motivator.

Many of the locals protested in German, a language nobody understood. You could see the anger in their faces when the posse searched every house on the town's main street.

Finally, they rode out in all directions looking for signs of the James Gang, but none were found. Somehow the gang's tracks ended in Fredericksburg. There was no sign of their prey.

Marshal Thorn wondered what he had missed. If it had been up to him, the last thing he would have done was ride into town pell-mell and ready for a shootout. That was some reckless marshaling. It appeared Marshal Hard Talk lived up to his name. Then again, maybe he should be called Foolish Talk.

In the back of Thorn's mind was the fuzzy face of the shoeshine man. Although he shined his shoes at the time, he didn't even look at him. Maybe he was slipping a little. He was so focused on seeing Jesse and Frank that he forgot to look for anybody else. He wondered if they were being watched by the gang at that very moment.

JED LAY on a blanket with his Sharps rifle shouldered on a hill nearly eight hundred yards away. He levered a round into the chamber and looked down the scope. He counted seven or eight men. It was hard to tell because they rode into town like they were attacking a Rebel regiment. It took minutes for the dust clouds to settle. They were scaring the dickens out of the locals. Women dropped what they had in their hands and ran for their lives. The lawmen were scaring them more than if Jesse and Frank had ridden into town with the Younger brothers in tow.

Children watched the spectacle from under the boardwalk. All that could be seen were the whites of their eyes as they propped their chins in their hands and blinked. Horses' hooves clomped before their faces.

John, Jed, and Jodi had circled around town and followed an overgrown and treacherous trail. They knew Jesse and Frank wouldn't stop in the most obvious place. They had skirted Austin and rode up to Fredericksburg; they turned and backtracked to throw the posse off. It wasn't like their pursuit wasn't expected. That was clear as soon as the shootout went down in the hotel in San Antonio.

Instead of running right behind the James Gang, John, Jed, and Jodi hid in the poorest area of San Antonio, allowing John to get behind the posse. They tracked them as they trailed the rest of the outlaws. Even Jesse didn't know they were there.

"Whatcha wanna do here, John?" Jed asked. "You want me to wing a couple of 'em, or should I just shoot a horse or two?"

"Let's wait for a spell and see what they do," John said as he zeros in with his spyglass.

He had the head marshal in his sights. There was no mistaking who was giving orders to the rest. The marshal that followed them from El Paso was sitting on his horse at the edge of town, acting as if he knew they wouldn't find the James Gang there.

"It looks like the marshal that was on our tail has lost his job," Jed said.

"Looks can be deceiving," John replied. "He sure ain't as reckless as that bunch he brought with him. I doubt he be too happy right about now."

They watched and waited until finally, the posse saw the James brothers had tricked them again; they were nowhere to be found. Jed and John looked down from a hill, invisible to the men in town. Finally, the posse dismounted, tied their horses to the hitching rails and went into the saloon.

"Shoot the post, Jed. If you can bust up the posts on the hitching rail, you may be able to spook the horses. Need 'em to pull loose and run off. They'll find 'em soon enough and be plumb worn out. That will wear them out more than they already are, making it impossible for them to backtrack and follow the boys."

John and Jed stuffed cotton wads in their ears as Coal prepared to shoot. He sent a high-caliber buffalo round toward the hitching post. It slammed into the wood sending splinters flying. The horses panicked as their eyes spread wide and they fought to get free.

Somebody poked their head out the window, and Jed

put a well-placed round into a porch post near the door. Whoever it was, they disappeared immediately. A few more shots and the post were blown to smithereens. The horses tore their reins loose and squealed as they ran for the end of town and around the end of the last buildings. They disappeared in the dust cloud that followed them.

"That should do it," John said as he got to his feet.

Jed kept an eye on his scope, waiting to see the face of the bravest man in the building. That would be the leader. To his surprise, the marshal from El Paso sat astride his horse at the other end of town and stared in Jed's direction. He must have seen the gun smoke from so many bullets. He knew they were there, and they were tangled in a complicated game of cat and mouse.

John wondered what he, Jodi and Jed should do next. He knew the James brothers would head for home, where they could hide out with friends and family for months before anybody could find them. He had an idea of where that would be. Missouri was a big state. John planned for him, Jed, and Jodi to be long gone and in the opposite direction.

"You ever been to New Mexico or maybe Arizona?" John asked Jed and Jodi. "I've always dreamed of goin' farther west, maybe even California."

"I went to Santa Fe once with my pa to buy cattle," Jodi said.

"You know where I been and ain't been, John," Jed said. "Whatcha gettin' at?"

John thought if he followed the path just the same as in his youth, he might feel invincible. He wanted to cheat death, just as he did when he was enslaved. If they got far enough away from the war, maybe—just maybe—they could live free. First, they would have to get some more money, but they knew how to rob banks. Soon they would have the money they needed to get as far away as California or even Oregon, places where people had never heard of Capt. Quantrill and what his men had done.

CHAPTER 10

JODI GOODNIGHT

THAT NIGHT JODI SAT IN THE DARK, AT THE EDGE OF LIGHT provided by their campfire. She played mumble-peg dangerously close to her foot. The tension in her shoulders showed her displeasure. It wasn't a wave of anger you could put your finger on, but she was boiling mad. Repeatedly, she tried to get Jed Coal for her own, but something or somebody from his past always seemed to tear him away from her. Now it was that blasted Jesse James. She could hardly tolerate being around him. She could feel the evil come off him like waves of heat from a stove. She hated it when he mockingly flirted with her. If he ever touched her, she thought she would die.

Again, the James Gang was interfering in their attempt to make a life for themselves. John was a free man and moving toward being wealthy just like Jed. Jodi intended to plan the best bank robbery ever. They need one big score so they could run away, change their names, and become other people, ordinary folks with normal lives. She wanted them to be like most everybody else.

Three years ago; her father was still alive, and they were thriving on the ranch in the Texas Hill Country. How did the world change so much in such a short time? She had never really loved a man before Jed. Of course, she was younger than him, not that it mattered. The problem was he was an outlaw. Like her, she knew he was what he was due to no decisions of his own. When forced into the life like Jed and John endured, there was no choice but to ride it out the best you can. Lucky for them, they survived the war. Now, they only had to endure the aftermath.

Jodi turned and called over her shoulder, "Is there some room over there by the fire?"

"Only if'n you put that knife away," John said and snickered.

"Why are men so complicated?" Jodi asked as she stared straight at Jed Coal and took a seat on the log beside him.

Jed returned her gaze, puzzled. He had long ago forgotten what it was like to live like an average person. For him, this was normal. He had been living like this long enough that all the rest was just a foggy part of his brain. Even when he went there to look, it was difficult to recall; normality was just a misty ghost in his mind. So, when Jodi talked about such things, he listened but never pondered on the future long enough to worry. He knew what lay ahead. He had known for a long time.

Just the same, Jed was happy to be with Jodi, even if she was complicated. Most often, there wasn't time for moments alone or endearments. They were on the run again, and none of them knew for how long. They didn't even know if they would ever make it to California like John wanted. Jed had given up dreaming. Expectations were dangerous in his world, and hope could be an enemy.

It was safer to keep your guard up, focus on the situation, and not expect anything good. Hope provided more disappointment. He had done that day in and day out for four years during the Civil War and never had a day off. It was a constant battle—ambush the enemy, flee south to Texas to recuperate and ride north again to wreak havoc.

Right now, the law was close—real close. There was no time to daydream about happier days. Today was what it was, and Jed accepted it, as did John Washington. It was Jodi who had not lived through what they had. So, she would never understand what they had done and seen. She would never truly know them. Jed thanked God for that.

"So, ya wanna head west, do ya?" Jed asked. "At this point, one way is as good as another as long as it ain't behind Jesse and Frank."

"I have a better idea," Jodi said.

The fire crackled and popped as green branches bubbled and spewed steam. Cinders swirled skyward on thermal currents as smoke rose and disappeared into the night. Flames lashed out at the dark, dancing in their eyes. Coyotes sang their nightly chorus as an owl hooted and another replied. The night was warm, and the light was a soft silver from a half moon. Shadows stood long against cactus as the three huddled together, as Miss Goodnight told them her plan.

~

MARSHAL THORN SAT astride his horse at the edge of Fredericksburg and wondered what was really going on. Had they been led there to be bushwhacked? That was the Raiders' specialty. If the man shooting the gun wanted to hit somebody, he clearly could have. As far as Thorn could see, all his shots were well-placed and accurate. There was nothing shabby about his work.

The San Antonio lawmen were chasing down the horses, which would, of course; be baked. He knew what Marshal Talk would want to do. That wasn't necessarily what the outlaws were going to do, though. There was an inkling inside telling him they had a different plan. He believed the James Gang probably would head home to avoid being caught.

The old lawman in him must have given him that gut feeling. He now was focusing on the Black man. Thorn figured it must be him and his thin friend. The girl must be with the White man. Who she was, he couldn't say or care. He decided two members of the James Gang would do. He just had to figure out what they would do next and how he could catch them unawares. It would be difficult.

The posse thought they had the gang trapped, but they weren't where they thought they would be. They seemed to be a few steps ahead of them at every turn. They clearly knew a posse was on their tail. They even knew about Marshal Thorn—that much was obvious. What else did they know that they shouldn't, he wondered?

He watched as Marshal Talk stormed up and down the street while the rest of the men were out running down the horses. Unfortunately, these were the best horses they could get. The marshal proposed the locals' loan horses to the posse. The Germans weren't having any of it, though. Without cash, the posse would get squat. What if they were killed in the process? Then the ranchers would be out their horses and money.

Again, Marshal Thorn knew they had to head back out before the tracks got cold. If a good breeze blew up or it rained, that would be all she wrote. The San Antonio lawman believed if he pushed both the animals and the men, they could still catch them. Nobody ever got away from Hard Talk—at least, not until now. Billy Bob had doubts about the San Antonio marshal's abilities.

Marshal Talk knew they all were tired, both the men and the horses. He believed they had enough life left in them to make that last stretch of land to catch the outlaws. The San Antonio marshal could taste the victory; it was so close. If he caught or killed even one of the James Gang, his name would go down in history. He had already been a famous officer in the Civil War.

The problem was he was on the losing side so and his commendations meant little to the new Yankee power in charge. If he caught one or both brothers, he would again bathe in the glory of victory. He would see his name again in the newspapers, just like during the war. This time he would be on the winning side, though. He had learned his lesson. Before going off half-cocked, it was best to be clever in picking and choosing a side to fight for. It was best if you carefully selected the winner.

Dogs barked as horses' hooves pounded the earth. The rest of the posse was returning with the runaway horses.

Marshal Thorn remained outwardly as passive as he could while his concerns grew on several fronts. He pursed his lips as he stared into the distance, thinking about all the different ways he could go about capturing at least part of the gang. He disrespected, disliked, and felt no loyalty to Marshal Talk. He wasn't the well-balanced hard male he made himself out to be. He was a butcher, looking for a slaughter.

On the other hand, Billy Bob was possibly one of the most mentally healthy, well-balanced lawmen left in Texas. Thorn was very different than Marshal Talk. He never cussed in anger or used animated gestures or wild facial expressions. He was always even and steady. He had a calm, analytical way that made him always appear at ease. When Marshal Talk climbed astride his horse and stormed his way, he waited with an expressionless face. He was curious about what the marshal had to say but had no intention of continuing with him. The man would never find the James Gang unless they wanted him to. Then, it would be too late. They would have the posse in their sights and be shot dead in seconds.

Sure, Marshal Talk was an officer in the war, but Thorn wasn't fooled by all his swagger and bravado. Billy Bob had no intention of letting the man guide him to his own slaughter.

Talk pulled to a sliding stop next to Thorn and bellowed, "Well, whatcha waitin' on, Thorn? Ya gonna sit here all day long?"

Billy Bob sucked on his quid and spat a yard of brown juice at the feet of the city marshal's horse. He tipped his hat, wheeled his horse around and trotted off without a word. He was done wasting his breath on the old fool. He would either end up lost in the rugged country that lay ahead or end up shot and killed if he managed to find the James Gang.

"Where do you think you're going?" Marshal Talk growled. "Get your tail back here right now. We're gonna run those dogs to ground and kill 'em all."

Thorn gigged his horse to hasten its pace and left Talk behind, swearing at his back. He didn't even feel the need to give him an excuse. The debacle in Fredericksburg was enough for him; he wasn't interested in riding with foolish men. He would do better on his own.

When he looked back, he could see the dust cloud from the posse as they rode south again. Thorn turned back in his saddle and continued to head east.

CHAPTER 11

AUSTIN, TEXAS

AUSTIN WAS BUSY WHEN JODI, JED, AND JOHN RODE INTO town. All three were dressed well and looked more like businesspeople than outlaws. That was the point. They checked into the Cherry Tree Hotel, located in the middle of town and across from the savings and loan on the corner. They got a suite on the second floor with double doors onto the balcony. It gave them a perfect view of the Wells Fargo Bank right next to the Austin Saving and Loan. It was a moonless night sky. Many of the lights in town were out, so they didn't attract summer bugs.

Jed ran his hand through his shaggy hair and looked at Jodi. Then he scanned the buildings across the street and to his left. John did the same to his right. Coal took another drag on his hand-built. The cinder glowed orange on his face. They had no desire to get too close to anybody other than the three of them. They used to do that in the war, too. It was more accessible to mourn a person you didn't know than a close friend. They had no idea where Jesse and Frank had gone. Hopefully, they were well north of them, which would be the last they saw of the brothers.

Despite their differences, they *were* all like brothers. If Jesse or Frank died, it would deeply hurt both Jed and John. Jesse's demise would be the most difficult to accept because he had always seemed indestructible. They knew one day he would meet his end, though. Whether it was sooner or later remained to be seen. At any rate, it would be better if it happened far away, and they didn't have to watch or maybe die with them.

They all knew their freedom was like a time bomb. It could go off at any moment, and they would all lose their lives. John clung to his dream of California and Jodi to her dream of a normal life with Jed. Coal knew the truth, though. He couldn't change the way he was any more than he could turn into a duck and fly. John just liked to dream of freedom. It started some years back and came true for everybody but John. Jed never dreamed of anything because his nights were full of nightmares and demons.

Jed and John shared a look. They both knew they were in unchartered waters. They were putting all their faith in Jodi's plan. It seemed crazy initially, but who would expect them to hit a bank so close right after losing the posse? Jodi figured Austin would be the last place the San Antonio marshal would look. Hopefully, they would get away with enough money to run for California if they could successfully pull off the heist. They all knew they were running on borrowed time. They also wished they knew where the James Gang went.

They took their supper on the porch, despite the insects. They were used to roughing it. So, no matter how you painted it, staying in a hotel was pure luxury for them. The building was painted white. Royal blue curtains festooned from the windows. A breeze kept them cool on the roof of the dining room. A bottle of fine Kentucky whiskey sat on the table between John and Jed. Jodi sat on Jed's lap as she hung her arms around his neck. Occasionally, she would surprise him and kiss his cheek.

Jed only let Jodi act like that when they were alone and with John. With all he had done and seen, he was still conservative in his views of certain things. Maybe he would change in the future. For some things, Jed was set in his ways. Showing affection publicly was one of them. He only allowed it on the second-floor porch because nobody on the street could see them.

John pulled out his spyglass and let it sweep across the glass windows of the banks below. Elegant white columns lined the entrance giving the impression of safety. The Wells Fargo Bank was new. The savings and loan appeared to have been there for many years. It might have been the first locally owned bank in town.

Jed watched the street over the brim of his glass. Jodi was so close he could smell her soap. She unpinned her long blond hair, so it fell to her shoulders, made eyes at her man and snuggled her head into his shoulder. For her, these short moments together were treasures. There were too many times when they were on the run and there was no time for romance. As much as she disliked it, she, of course, understood.

She watched as John peered into the dark corners of the street below them. She knew Jed, too, would be looking for trouble. They both had flipped a switch in their minds, so their actions were automatic. After years of running and ambushing the enemy, they had learned to take in things ordinary people don't see; their eyes always were searching. They knew the law was hot on their trail and could cross their path at any given moment. By now, more men could have joined the posse. Everybody wanted a piece of Jesse James.

ALL FIVE MEN filed into the barn in a way not much different from a herd of cows headed back to shelter after a day grazing in the pasture. Their heads were down. Their pace was slow and footing unsure. The only thing they had on their minds was sleep. The horses' lungs sounded like broken engines as they coughed and heaved; they were nearly baked.

The James Gang had managed to shake the posse by backtracking. Now, they had to decide what they wanted to do and where they wanted to go. They needed a rest and heal some wounds to their egos. Frank still didn't know how a lawman managed to follow them to San Antonio. The gang's elder member believed some of them were losing their touch. He whispered something to Jesse, and they both looked at Bob Younger. Jesse stifled a snicker.

Bob felt the shiner on his eye throb as his heart pounded between his ears. He hadn't been the same since the beating from Jed Coal. His one eye still looked off in another direction, leaving him off center. Sometimes he didn't know which eye to use. His brain struggled to capture two images at once.

His real problem was between his temples, where a psyche crack sent him to rarely visited places in the darkest corners of his memory. It was like a worm gnawing at the back of his head, crawling up his brain stem. He felt all the signs—quickened breathing, a tight chest, and the desire to flee. All were things he had never felt before. He was used to bullying men around. Now, his confidence seemed to have vanished.

Bob Younger loved to swear and drink and run after blemished doves. He knew his life was on a collision course with right and wrong. It was about to crash. An hour after their arrival, he was so drunk he launched into a symphony of flatulence for half an hour before slipping into a slumber. He snored loudly when he finally ran out of gas.

Frank stood beside the open barn door. He took a sip of whiskey and looked out across the countryside. He had had a half dozen drinks, but he wasn't drunk. When it came to liquor, as well as most things, he had the constitution of a man three times his size. His unshakable confidence was a bit shaky, too. He felt a nagging feeling of indecision. It was something that most people felt every day, but it was rare for him. He was a man who was used to being in complete control and right all the time. Uncertainty was an unwelcome feeling for the eldest James brother. He would rather be run over by a stagecoach than have his mind filled with doubt.

The barn they hid in belonged to an old friend with a debt to pay. He even offered them some horses he could spare. They weren't up to the gang's standards, but they would allow them to rest their horses. They would have to do for the time being.

"I ain't lost my step," Bob Younger said in an embarrassed voice as he suddenly startled and awoke. "I just underestimated Jed, is all. He tricked me is what he did."

He was still as drunk as a sailor.

"You might as well admit it," Jesse said and snickered. "Jed whooped ya fair and square. Why you hardly laid a hand on 'em. He was twice as fast as you. If you want some advice, I'd stay away from my buddy, Jed. He's a hard nail, he is."

Jessy grinned at Bob Younger, taunting him to sass back. He clearly didn't understand his limitations with Jed. He knew exactly where he stood with Jesse, though. Nobody messed with Jesse James and lived very long to talk about it. Frank was considerably more tolerant, and it was he who tried to dampen Jesse's wild side when it began to get out of control.

"Whatcha think we ought to do now?" Jesse asked. "I know ya wanna head back home, but I was thinking about leaving the posse a present."

"And what kind of present might that be?" Frank asked. "By now, they've backtracked to where we stopped leaving a trail. We forded four times between the rocky surface and the river; I doubt they know where the hell we've gone.

"That San Antonio sheriff thinks he's smarter than he really is. They know we wanna head north to hide out in Missouri, but I doubt they imagine us going east and robbing a bank in Austin on the way. It's always best to do the opposite the law thinks you're gonna do."

"I reckon that's as good a way to go as any," Frank replied. "That'll send the posse around in circles and give us a chance to pick some much-needed money. I hate to steal from the ranches along the trail home. I'd rather pay my way north than fight my way."

"Where do you think John and Jed went with the pretty blonde cowgirl?" Jesse asked.

"You best stop hackin' on Jed about that woman," Frank said. "You better stop flirtin' with her, too. It ain't right, and you know it. Jed ain't never done nothin' to you but save your bacon upon occasion. I'd have felt better if Jed and John had stayed with us. That man can shoot the eyeballs off a fly and John the wings. With them covering us from afar, I doubt there be a bank we couldn't rob and still get away. Just the way we used to do when we rode with Quantrill's Raider."

The Younger brothers heard what they said. Frank wasn't shy with his men. John, Jim, and Cole looked at the toes of their boots, but Bob just couldn't shut up. He was having a hard time accepting he was bested. They all knew he was a blowhard and a bully; not even his brothers took up for him. Cole was the closest Younger to the James brothers. He shook his head, embarrassed because his brother was being drunk and stupid again.

Cole usually played referee between the James brothers and Bob. Today he had no defense. Bob had asked for it, and he had gotten every lick he deserved. It was too bad about his dodgy eye, though. He hoped it would slip back into place so he could see where he was going without tripping over his feet. Cole doubted it would do his shooting aim too much good, either. Then again, he never was the best shot of the bunch. Every family had a parent, brother, or sister like Bob. Family was family, though. So Cole kept his mouth shut and hoped his brother would sober up before he said the wrong thing to Jesse.

WITHOUT KNOWING IT, both parties of outlaws were headed for Austin. Unbeknownst to Jed, John, and Jodi when they rode into town, the James Gang was already there. Both of them rode straight for the big city after losing the posse.

Nearly ten thousand people populated Austin, and it was growing hand over fist and attracted several banks to town. There was also a high population of freedmen. Nineteen percent of the population was Black. So, John blended right in. Jed and Jodi looked like any other young couple who built this city. Nobody seemed to notice them.

Just the same, they didn't venture out into the population. John was still concerned about part of the posse. Not the foolish marshal from the Bat Cave in San Antonio. He was concerned with the man who had followed them all the way from El Paso. The tenacity of the lawman was second to none, and John had the sneaking feeling he wasn't done with them yet. He seemed like a dog after a bone. Until he got what he wanted, he would never give up. John wondered if he would try to follow them to California if he didn't locate them sooner.

"When ya wanna take the bank?" Jed asked Jodi. She whispered something into his ear, and they both laughed.

"First, you've got to decide which bank we wanna rob," John said.

"We can hit the Wells Fargo Bank," Jodi smiled. "The small one looks like an old local bank; if we rob it, these city folks may lose their savings. If we hit the Wells Fargo Bank, we'll hurt a few rich Yankees, and none of the poor folks will lose out."

"You sound more like Jesse every day," Jed jested. "You tryin' to make outlaws sound like the good guys?"

"It works for the James brothers," Jodi replied. "Maybe it'll work for us. It was the Wells Fargo Bank that took our farm back in Waco. My pa died, and I fell on hard times. The bank took it all, one plot at a time. It won't bother me none to take their money. It'll be a pleasure."

"So, how're we gonna go about doin' it?" John asked. "I hope you got some kind of plan."

"Tell him, Jed. I don't feel right doin' it," Jodi said.

"What is it, girl?" John smiled. "You can tell old Uncle John, can't cha?'"

Jed smiled and said, "She wants us to dress up so nobody will recognize us after we rob the bank. Oh, we can rob it easily enough, but the gettin' away is always the stickler."

"And how is that gonna work out?" John asked, puzzled.

"Jodi figured it would be best if we go in separate," Jed explained. "She's gonna go like a mourning widow and ask the bank what she should do with her recently deceased husband's money. Bankers always get sloppy when they're greedy. What better target than a crying widow? She's gonna wear a veil and all so nobody will get a good look at her face. She'll hide her pistols under her dress. You, my old friend, are going to accompany me and pretend I'm your master."

Jed had to laugh. John Washington had been his boss throughout the Civil War, and for the time they've been running together. He found the ruse entertaining.

John chuckled, then stopped and said, "But the wars over and the Black folks be free."

"It ain't been that long, and I've seen plenty of plantation owners in the South that resist," Jed said. "Some formerly enslaved people found better jobs; others stayed on with their old masters. Not many, though. Most moseyed along their own way. You know as well as I do some of the ornery plantation owners don't quite accept the loss of what they considered their property. Jodi said I should act like one of them. They all be rich anyway. Bankers love rich folks, especially these big banks with branches all over the country."

"We'll walk in like always, put a brace of pistols in their faces and take the money," Jodi said. "This time, when we make a break for it, we'll circle around, climb up the drainpipe and go in the back window of the hotel right across the street. Then, we'll cut your and Jed's hair and beards off and change our clothes. The only thing we need is some supplies for the first part of the journey. We'll be heading west for New Mexico, Arizona, Nevada and finally California. If we steal enough money on this job, we can retire. If not, we can lay low for the next few years until the heat blows over.

"We change our names as soon as we leave Texas. You and I are gonna be Mr. and Mrs. Smith, and John will be Mr. Jones," Jodi continued and laughed so loudly she had to hold her belly. "I couldn't think of more common names. I reckon that'll do it. Since nobody will know who we are, we can take our time. You boys get the horses, and I'll run by the general store, and we'll ride off into the sunset."

As she finished, Jodi smiled from ear to ear.

CHAPTER 12

MARSHAL HARD TALK

WHEN TALK'S POSSE ARRIVED AT THE END OF THE JAMES Gang's trail, they wandered aimlessly across a river and back, looking for tracks on the north and south banks. They found nothing. The six outlaws just up and vanished into thin air. The bad-tempered marshal whipped his horse, forcing it to ford the river again and again. The animal lunged up the riverbank when he gigged its flanks with his sharp, silver spurs, dropped to its knees and keeled over. He was as dead as dirt. Marshall Talk had ridden him to death. Like clockwork, one of the deputy's horses died next, just five minutes later.

Once the struggle was over and they stopped, the horses could hardly stay on their feet. Some dropped to the ground. Others moved about dazed and lethargic.

Talk looked down at his dead horse, began kicking the animal and yelled, "Get up, you stupid animal! You can't die on me now. We've almost got Jesse James!"

His men watched uncomfortably. This wasn't how a marshal after the James Gang was supposed to act. Their confidence in their leader began to wane. What would happen when they caught up with them and came face-to-face with Frank and Jesse? Then again, there were the Younger brothers, the Black man and the shootist. The outlaws seemed to be multiplying while their horses were dying like flies.

Sheriff Matt Hader called out, "If we don't get some fresh horseflesh, we ain't gonna catch nobody."

"But we've got to stay on their trail," Hard Talk barked like an Indian camp dog. "I ain't gonna let the James Gang get away when I'm so close."

"If we keep on like this, we're gonna have to walk," Hader retorted.

That was when Sheriff Hader's horse dropped out from under him, lay on the ground defeated and died. The Bat Cave sheriff swore as he pulled his pistol and put a bullet into its brain.

"You do what you wanna do, Marshal Talk," Hader roared. "I'm headin' with my deputies for Austin to collect some fresh horses. We need two each if we wanna catch up with these scoundrels."

The sheriff and his deputies wheeled their horses east. Marshal Talk didn't like it, but it was clear he had no choice. Austin would be the closest place to get good animals. Then they could resume the chase. He and his hired guns followed begrudgingly as their exhausted horses stumbled over their own hooves. Three were riding double. More horses would die before they made it to Austin. Hader thought it was a waste of good horse-flesh, but what was done was done. He could hardly blame Talk for everything.

The outlaws they were chasing were better than any he had ever pursued. From what he had read in the newspapers, he knew they were much more dangerous than most wanted men. The Youngers and the James brothers were known not to hesitate when facing the law. They made their own laws and shot marshals and sheriffs at a whim.

A man on a crusade always was the most dangerous, and the James brothers were on a religious-like campaign against rich banks and railroads. Harder didn't know much about the caliber of outlaws he chased but knew to tread very lightly. They could turn up when least expected and strike like a rattler. Jesse was said to be as fast as a viper with his guns. He was known for that and whistling lonely tunes when traveling at night. At least, that was what the dime novels said. Then again, most of what was printed was lies and fiction.

By the time the posse arrived at the outskirts of town, they were walking the few horses remaining because they continued to lose animals along the way. First went the horses that were ridden double. The lawmen walking could barely put one foot in front of another. They were covered from head to toe in trail dust, and their mouths were so dry their lips stuck to their teeth.

"I know you ain't gonna like it, Marshal, but my men need a night's sleep in a bed and a couple of healthy meals before the take after that wild bunch again," Hader said as he walked beside the Marshal Talk.

Hard Talk didn't like what he heard. With one look at his men, he could see if he insisted they push on, they would quit. Then, he would never capture or kill the James Gang; he'd lose his chance for fame. It would be national news, maybe even gain international headlines when he caught the Jesse Gang. It would be bigger than anything he had ever imagined. He nodded his head and bit his tongue so the words in his mind didn't walk out of his mouth and spoil everything.

~

WHEN THE POSSE limped into town, Hard Talk didn't notice Marshal Thorn camped in a stand of trees. He was just finishing for the day and would head into town the following morning. He had kicked this thing about the two shooters around in his head and started to believe he was wrong. They were probably long gone by now. They could have fled in any direction. He wondered why Marshal Talk was racing for Austin when the James Gang was headed for Missouri. He wondered what happened to all their horses.

Billy Bob had his sights set a little lower. If he could manage to bring the Black man back to stand trial again, along with the White shooter, he would have done his job. Jesse and Frank James were too anxious to fight and willing to kill. He thought maybe the other two would be more reasonable, especially with the blonde cowgirl with them.

Suddenly, it dawned on him. If he could manage to capture the White woman, he could probably barter her life for theirs. Thorn smiled so wide his molars showed. His eyes lit up like he just saw his next move in a chess game. Hunting outlaws was all about moving pieces across the board until you had the villain trapped—in a real-life checkmate. The cowgirl was the answer to the puzzle. With her, he knew he wouldn't be shot. Her man would be too worried a stray bullet would hit her. Even if he was shot his muscle reflex would suffice to pull the trigger and the blonde would die.

Sure, there were still things to work out. If they were in the city, where would they be? There were several hotels and dozens of bars.

Then it suddenly dawned on him. If they were in Austin, they would be casing out another bank. Why else come east when the safest way to run would be north, west, or south? There couldn't be more than three or four saving and loans for a population of ten thousand.

He rummaged in his memory for large, modern banks that were located in the city. He knew the town well because he had brought numerous outlaws from El Paso to Austin to hang. Big banks seemed to be the ones the James Gang had targeted up until now; they would be the banks with the most money. It made sense to rob banks with the most gold and silver. Why take the same risk for a lesser sum?

He walked the streets of Austin and located the Wells Fargo Bank beside a small local saving and loan. He walked to the edge of town and found another bank that was only a block from the trail out of Austin. It looked like a perfect place to rob because of the nearby escape route. It was an older bank, but it probably held enough money for the James Gang to get back home to Missouri. It would be much safer to rob than the big bank in the middle of the city. He took a seat on a saloon porch a few doors down from the savings and loan so he could keep an eye on things.

He ordered a whiskey-laced coffee and pulled out a worn rosewood pipe. He fished in his pocket for a small pouch of sweet-smelling tobacco and tapped the bowl full. He lit a match and puffed until red cinders glowed in the middle. Billows of smoke swirled around his head as he gazed across the street.

The sun blazed overhead, baking the country from one end of the state to the other. Waves of heat could be seen in the distance. Cactus trees wavered in the heat, and cicadas continued with their noisy racket. From somewhere along this end of the street came the smell of freshly made cornbread and frying bacon. Billy Bob puffed his pipe like a teapot smokestack on a Baldwin locomotive.

Just as he lifted his coffee to his lips, he spotted Marshal Talk and his men positioned around the bank. The problem was there were so many now it was impossible for all of them to remain hidden. The discipline of the posse left much to be desired, Thorn thought. It looked like Marshall Talk had more deputies than before, and the street was lined with good quality horseflesh. He could only assume the posse was waiting on the James Gang to show up. Strings of unsaddled horses lined the adjoining alley. Talk's men weren't taking any chances of being set afoot again.

Billy Bob thought the Black man and the shooter would show if he got lucky. He doubted the James Gang would be so bold as to stick around for so long. Then again, it was Jesse James, and there was no telling what that man would do. Thorn debated on whether to cross the street and have a word with Hard Talk or not. He decided to stay where he was and continue his surveillance. He didn't like that oafish San Antonio marshal anyway.

It was better if he sat alone instead of with Talk's group of misfits. Most of the men appeared to be gunslingers and bounty hunters. They all had stars on their chests because they were deputized; that didn't mean they had an ounce of honesty in them. Thorn guessed that's why they appeared so disorganized. Their egos were so big, nobody would listen to anybody else.

He had to figure out how to get the two outlaws with the blonde woman before the posse did. Then, he might just be able to control the situation. If the big city marshal stepped in, surely there would be bloodshed. Thorn was going to try to do this by the book.

Of course, if the James Gang showed up to rob a bank, Marshal Talk was more than welcome to that confrontation. It might just be the diversion he needed to get out of town with the two outlaws he was after.

Thorn decided he would worry about how he got them back to El Paso without getting shot later. At the moment, he had to catch them first. That, too, could be fraught with danger.

Frank and Jesse might be gone already, but the other two could shoot the whiskers off a field mouse at five hundred yards. As he watched, he suddenly began to think about the Wells Fargo Bank. Just because this bank was an easy target, didn't mean the James Gang or the two shooters gave a rat's ass about the added danger.

He downed his coffee and hammered his pipe on his palm, so tobacco fell onto the floor. He stuffed it back in his pocket, pulled the brim of his hat down low, and headed for the center of Austin and the Wells Fargo Bank. It was a long shot, but he figured as soon as the outlaws saw the posse poorly hidden all over that side of the street, they would change plans. Especially with a dozen fresh horses saddled and ready at the hitching rails and another dozen grazing on what grass they could find in the shadow-filled alley.

The horses pulled at tufts of grass and slid their jaws as they whisked their tails against the flies. They neighed and nickered as they ate. Even an occasional snort was heard. The saddled horses stood shoulder to shoulder next to the bank and in front of a grain store.

As soon as the San Antonio lawmen were out of sight, Billy Bob began to run. He had a feeling he had picked the wrong bank. His arms pumped like a locomotive.

In his mind's eye, he saw the Wells Fargo robbery. Why hadn't he seen it before? Was it too late? Would the outlaws have vanished already? He would only know when he arrived at the new location in the center of town.

He was two blocks away when he saw three people exit the hotel's front door. The hotel was across from the bank, and they ran for the alley across the street. Thorn felt the teeth of failure biting at his heels.

If only he could get close enough to grab the girl. Then something he didn't expect happened. The blonde cowgirl split off from the men with the satchels. They headed in a different direction.

Billy Bob Thorn wasn't a fool. He knew the men from Quantrill's Raiders would have him for breakfast in a face-to-face fight. Men who could shoot like that with rifles were usually proficient with their pistols, too. He had a feeling they both were more than average, or they wouldn't have survived.

He pulled his hat down, wrapped his hand around his pistol grip, and roared across the street, leaving a wake of dust trailing behind. The two ex-soldiers vanished; Thorn let them go. He needed to keep his eyes on the cowgirl. Finally, he saw her stop on the boardwalk. She looked all around and ducked into a general store, providing him the opportunity he needed. He looked over his shoulder, expecting to see her friends. It was nothing but a flare of paranoia. He told himself to calm down, or he would blow it this time. He pulled his gun, put his back against the wall next to the door and waited. He could hear his heart hammering between his ears, as sweat formed under his arms.

Streaks of sweat streamed down his face turning the mud to dirt leaving white tracks on his cheeks. His breath came fast and short. His knuckles turned white as he unconsciously squeezed his pistol grip. It seemed to take forever for the woman to come back out. Maybe she had ducked out the back door, he thought.

No, be patient. Stand your ground or you'll lose your last chance at the outlaws.

CHAPTER 13

SURPRISES

JODI HAD JUST DUCKED INTO THE STORE TO BUY SOME DRY goods for their escape. She bought salted pork, beans, flour, sugar, tobacco, coffee, and some sweets. She finished up with a few more items, paid the man behind the counter and turned to leave. Jed and John would be waiting for her with the horses three blocks down in the alley's shadows. The bank job had gone perfectly, just like Jodi had planned. Nobody would imagine they were the same people who robbed the Wells Fargo Bank.

She sucked on a red, white, and green candy cane as she turned for the exit. She had to smile to herself. The James Gang was supposed to be the top dogs when it came to robbing banks. Jodi had to differ with them. She not only robbed banks but also did it so the victims didn't know who the robbers were. Dressed in her riding clothes, she was ready to head for California. It looked like they were going to make it after all. Even if Jed never believed it, she and John had kept the faith. In the end, they would get there.

She passed the fancy silk and satin material as she

moved toward the door. She let her hand slip across the fabrics. They were so smooth and soft. Maybe one day, she would have a dress made of silk. Money would not be an obstacle. Bright colors filled her eyes with wonder. When she got to California, that would be what she would do. She would have a white silk wedding gown, just like the city's wealthy folks. She believed once they hit California, Jed Coal would be ready to marry her. Of course, Uncle John would always have a place in their home.

In a flash, she looked back on everything thing that happened in the last months. She was surprised to find herself with such unusual companions. Never in her life did she dream she would fall in love with an outlaw, or make friends with the likes of Quantrill's Raiders. Just the name instilled fear in most men. She knew a different side of both of these ex-soldiers, though. They were dangerous, not doubt, but beneath that rough facade there were two good men who were dealt a bad hand that changed their lives forever.

Jumping over a broom wasn't going to make it for Miss Jodi Goodnight. Mrs. Smith sounded so common she felt it was perfect. All she wanted to do was blend in with the rest of the world. Jodi had drawn enough attention to last her a lifetime. She had been lucky so far; nobody knew who she was and what she had done. She wondered what the Pacific Ocean looked like. She had seen the Gulf of Mexico and wondered if they would look the same or be the same color.

She had no idea what California would be like, but it sounded grand just the same. She had never even read a thing about it. Until John Washington brought it up, California never crossed her mind. Now, she felt it was the perfect solution. If the long arm of the law reached that far, they always could go south to Mexico, north to Canada or catch a ship in San Francisco and sail off to some faraway land where they weren't known. With a good heist, they could go anywhere they wanted. She had heard of an island on the other side of the world. It was called Australia. Would that be far enough away, she wondered?

When she walked out the door, a man appeared to one side and shoved his pistol barrel in her side. Jodi froze on the spot. She turned her head and saw the star over his heart. Sunlight flashed off the tin making her squint.

"I don't wanna shoot ya, ma'am. Just come along with me, and you'll be just fine. My name is Marshal Thorn out of El Paso. I reckon you know well enough how long I've been chasin' y'all. I ain't interested in you now, girl. I just want the Black fella that escaped from the court-house and his friend. You know, the one that's so good with that rifle of his."

"Do you really think I'm gonna tell you where my friends are so you can shoot them down?" Jodi spat. "Go ahead and shoot me. I double dare ya."

Billy Bob was confused. The cowgirl was supposed to fear the law. She didn't seem to be frightened at all, not even with a pistol in her back. What was he thinking? He expected her to be an innocent girlfriend. Instead, he suddenly realized she was an outlaw, too. His knuckles turned white as he squeezed the grip on the pistol even harder. His mind swirled and he sought the way forward. He drew back the hammer so she could hear the chamber click and know he was serious.

To his surprise, she cursed, kicked, punched, and

yanked as hard as she could to get free, never heeding the gun. Finally, without a choice, he thumped her on the head with the barrel. She dropped to the ground like a sack of beans. He finally breathed a sigh, part resignation and part relief.

There was no turning back now. Jodi wasn't unconscious but stopped struggling and shuddered at the thought of the danger she could be putting Jed and John in. She had to do something to stop the marshal from finding them. She knew she wouldn't talk. If he had found her, maybe he could find Jed and John too. Then she would lose them both forever.

JED AND JOHN waited for Jodi with the loot they had stolen from the Wells Fargo Bank. They had her spotted horse saddled and ready to go. Four extra horses were on leads. One would carry the supplies and stolen money. After minutes passed, Jed began to get nervous. John admonished him, pulled a tobacco plug from his pocket and cut the tip off with his knife. He popped the quid into his cheek. He was as calm as the day was long. Usually, Jed was that way, too, but he was falling for the Waco cowgirl. Washington could see it in his eyes, especially when they returned from that short spell alone. Jed worried now, something they never did during the war. Once the fighting started, there wasn't any time to worry.

It was the first time he had seen him at peace since he met Jed as a young sniper. That was when the captain ordered him into their detail. He, like John, had no sayso in the matter. It looked like they had little to say in the course of their lives. Until now, everything had been decided for them, be it for good or bad. Finally, Jed had something to lose, thus his concern. Worry always accompanied love.

Of course, Jed and John took care of each other throughout the Civil War, but it wasn't the same. They assumed they were both walking dead men until the day it was over. Neither one expected to ride away from that hell. Luckily, they vanished. Now, they had to repeat the vanishing act and lose themselves in California.

"Where can that woman be?" Jed asked as he peeked around the corner and onto the busy street. Beads of sweat rolled down his face. "It's not like her to be late." Underneath Jed's bronzed face, his cheeks flushed, and his brow furrowed. He couldn't hide his worry and concern.

"I reckon we best go see what's holdin' her up," John said, spitting a gob of chew on the ground.

"And leave the money here?" Jed asked. "What about the extra horses? Jodi never strays off her plan. You stay here, and I'll go find her. If you hear shootin' hightail it out of here. At least you'll have the money."

"I'm sorry, Jed, but you and Jodi are more important to me than the money," John said. "We can always steal more gold and silver. Let's take a chance and hide the loot under the building here, and I can sneak back later tonight and get it. Chances are nobody will find it. We'll be too obvious if we try to carry four big satchels down Main Street. We walked out of that bank not an hour ago."

"All right then," Jed said as he climbed atop his horse.

He grabbed the reins of Jodi's horse and walked them into the street. He wheeled them to the right and into light traffic. There were people on Main Street and nobody paid them much attention. When they rode past the Wells Fargo Bank, they noticed city constables inside with the tellers and the manager. Nobody noticed them in their fine duds and with clean-shaven faces. They even cut their hair. They looked like a couple of travelers passing through. The only hint of trouble was the riderless horse—Jodi's horse.

"The problem ain't gonna go away until we send those lawmen a message they won't forget," Jed spat. He was beginning to get angry. Soon somebody was going to pay if something happened to Jodi. "I intend to get revenge."

John swallowed hard as he considered the possibilities. Where could she have gone? Jodi was supposed to go buy supplies and head straight to the waiting horses. She wasn't back in the bank with the law, or they would have seen her.

"Revenge? I prefer the word retribution. Of course, it all depends on the definition you use. Revenge is wild and less calculated and very personal," John whispered as though he was divulging secrets.

"And retribution?" Jed asked.

John thought for a moment before giving him an answer. "Retribution is a morally right and rightfully deserved punishment manifested by horribly, violent men—like us."

"You shouldn't talk such nonsense," Jed retorted.

A casualness about Jed Coal's exterior helped mask his complex being. Only John really knew how complicated he was.

John pulled his horse to a stop and backed up. Jed looked at John and asked, "What's wrong?"

Then he saw it, too.

"Crap," Jed huffed. "We've gotta get her back and quick."

Jed felt his stomach twist into a wrenching knot. Right in front of the general story sat Jodi with the marshal from El Paso beside her. It was hard to see, but Jed saw part of the gun barrel poking her in the side.

When Jodi saw the two of them, she nearly blurted out their names. Instead, she bit her tongue. The more attention they drew to themselves, the riskier it got. When she looked at Jed's face, it was like she never saw him before. It was foreboding; violence oozed from his pores.

This was a man she had not seen until now. He was so angry she could see a vein pulsate at his temple half a block away when his eyes locked on the marshal. She could feel his anger when he realized her dilemma.

Billy Bob Thorn's life passed before him. He suddenly realized he had made a mistake that might cost him dearly. Before, he was after two outlaws and did what he knew was right. Now, he had made it personal. He quickly noticed the difference in the shooter. Had he bitten off more than he could chew?

The rider came straight for him. If he was afraid, he sure as hell didn't show it. He appeared to be hell-bent on killing somebody. That somebody was Billy Bob Thorn because he had taken his woman. The marshal felt stupid and small. He was no better than Hard Talk. Both of them were all talk and no game. Now he felt foolish, but what was done was done. He couldn't take it back.

The outlaws pulled their horses up facing the marshal. Both men's faces looked like they had gazed into the deepest depths of Hades. Jed's voice was low and soft—it dropped to funeral depths.

"If you don't unhand my woman, I'm gonna fill you so full of holes they'll have to shovel ya into a wheelbarrow," he growled as his eyes burned into Thorn's.

Marshal Thorn seemed mesmerized by the man in front of him. He had never seen someone so terrifying in his life. He had seen him before, but he appeared quiet and calm. Now the shootist was anything but calm. He was there to wreak the wrath on the man who dared lay a hand on his girl.

When the pain struck, the marshal's eyes spread wide, and he opened his mouth to yell, but the blade of the knife was firm against his groin, and he didn't dare move. She wasn't wearing a gun. He never imagined a pretty, young woman carried a knife.

Jodi leaned in close and whispered in his ear, "You move, and I'll emasculate you with the flick of my wrist. You're out of your league, Marshal. What's going on here ain't for amateurs and small-town marshals and sheriffs. This is the big league, mister, and we run the show. If you doubt me, just try and make a move. I'll slice you like a stuck pig. I ain't the easy-goin' girl you think I am."

"The name's Marshal Billy Bob Thorn," he replied, his voice cracking with fear. His mouth was so dry it felt like it was full of sand. "I was just tryin' to do my job, ma'am."

When the James Gang rushed by, they didn't even notice Jed, John, and Jodi at the side of the road with Thorn. Right behind them rode the San Antonio marshal and three deputies. It looked like things went terribly wrong down the street. They all were surprised to see the James Gang ride down the road in full view. Everybody noticed the number of posse members had been reduced. All of the James Gang seemed unscathed. Of course, they were professional warriors with years of daily practice killing. That was something a local sheriff or marshal couldn't say.

Marshal Thorn immediately knew he was done. He was so far out of his league he would be lucky if they didn't kill him right then and there. The White shooter was angry enough to do it.

The marshal's gun clattered to the floor, and he raised his hands in the air. Jodi gave her wrist a little flick; the knife immediately drew blood. She, too, was as angry as hell at the intrepid lawmen. The man's audacity to capture her and hold her hostage like so much livestock was more than she could tolerate. He winced when the knife cut his skin, and a rivulet of blood ran down his leg. She only nicked him, but she could have just as easily slit his artery and killed him. He had suddenly realized what she was capable of.

When she stood, she grinned at the lawman with one hand on her cocked hip. She reached over and kissed him on the cheek. Red lipstick marked his face, embarrassing him further.

"It's not every day you succeed in surviving bank robberies with the James Gang in the mix," Jodi said with a cocky smirk. "If I were you, I'd hightail it back to El Paso before you get shot and killed like most of those San Antonio deputies."

Thorn just nodded his head. He couldn't take his eyes off Jed Coals. He felt if he looked away, he might snatch his life away quicker than a man could swat a fly. Jodi strolled off the porch with an arrogant swagger.

"We best chase after the San Antonio sheriff," John said. "We don't want 'em to shoot one of the boys."

Next, he turned to the marshal and said, "You best count your blessings, Thorn. This is the only chance I'm gonna give ya to walk away and go home to your job and family. So what? You didn't catch the James Gang. Half the law in the country is after them and can't catch 'em. You ain't done as bad as that dumb fool that's chasing the boys right now."

"If we stand here jawing all day, we ain't gonna get a chance to fend off the posse so Jesse and Frank can get away," Jed said.

Just hearing the James brothers' names made the marshal uneasy. Now that he had seen the kind of violence these men brought, Thorn was just about ready to resign and get another job. Time would tell when he got back to El Paso. That is, if he ever did get back home again. The way things had been looking lately, it was becoming doubtful.

Jodi ran for her horse and jumped astride in a single bound. Jed passed her the pistol and holster she normally wore, and they wheeled their horses for the other end of town and the posse. Maybe they could do the brothers one last favor to make all debts even.

Nobody was on the street. It looked like a ghost town when minutes before it was full of people. The fear the names Frank and Jesse James instilled into the citizens was amazing. Nobody wanted to get shot by the outlaws or from friendly fire. The trio raced away unchecked. Not a single gun barrel was visible all along the street. They could see two dust clouds in the distance. One was that of the fleeing James Gang; the other was the posse. A third cloud followed the three out of town.

John flashed a glance at Jed, which was all that was needed. They veered off and headed for the nearest high ground they could find. Jodi raced to keep up, but they left her in the dust. There was no hesitation. Time was running out.

Once they had a good blind to shoot from John got them in his spyglass and began to give Jed instructions. Both men had their Sharps rifles loaded and ready. Jed placed the barrel of his rifle in a handmade bipod. John pulled a tuft of grass and let it fall. The breeze had dropped to nothing. All Jed had to do was compensate for the height and distance. He closed one eye, stared down the scope, and got his first target in sight.

The muzzle jumped, and when it came back down, Jed was looking at a perfect shot. The horse under the deputy chasing Frank and Jesse dropped like a sack of flour. Jed squeezed the trigger again. The next bullet struck the second target. The third shot hit the marshal's horse, leaving three men horseless in seven seconds. Jed could place a bullet in a six-inch circle at eight hundred yards. There wasn't a better shot in the entire Confederate army. Several spent cartridges lay in a neat pile beside his right arm.

John was reloading Jed's weapon when he turned his head and looked over his shoulder. Leaning against a big oak a distance away stood the man who had been watching them back in Eagles Pass—the lawman who snatched Jodi. He was in the shade of the trees and Jed couldn't confirm who he was, but he felt it in his bones. He had no doubt it was the marshal from El Paso. Jed intended to put a bullet in his head if he was there when they were done with the posse. He had warned him and let him go when Jodi had him dead to rights.

Jed sent two more bullets spiraling out of the Sharps and into the horse flesh under the lawmen. He would have preferred to shoot the men rather than their horses. But there were some things the law just wouldn't overlook. Jed knew if he killed all the lawmen, they would regroup in San Antonio and come after them again. If he shamed them enough, they might call it quits.

Finally, the only man visible was Hard Talk. He was returning fire in their direction. His Winchester rounds fell far short; even if they hit Jed, they probably wouldn't kill him. He knew the buffalo gun would be a whole different story. The hammer fell with a click, and an explosion occurred in the chamber and sent a lead slug spiraling through the air toward Marshal Hard Talk. When the bullet hit him, it knocked him off his feet and threw him three yards back. It looked like a giant hand picked him up and slammed him against a wall. He slid to the wood plank floor, leaving a swipe of blood down the wall.

He still breathed, gasping for air as his left lung struggled to work. He seemed to be saying something as his lips moved, but nobody was there to hear him.

Marshal Hard Talk took one last breath and said, "Newspaper...Jesse James..." Then he died. Three of his deputies survived but were now riding pell-mell for the hills. They planned to get as far away as possible from the James Gang. They had seen enough of the deadly outlaws. Never again would they sign up for a posse.

When Jed was done with the San Antonio posse, John passed him a loaded rifle. He turned his gun toward the marshal with the black hat—Marshal Billy Bob Thorn. When Jed used his scope to trace across the distance, the marshal was no longer visible. He had seen the carnage of the shootist and finally retreated. Or had he? If a man chased them from El Paso to Eagles Pass, San Antonio and finally to Austin, how far would he chase them? Jed spat and swore. He should have shot him when he had the chance. He was busy with the posse, though.

Now, he would have to look over his shoulder all the time, wondering if the tenacious lawman was still on their trail. They remounted, rode west for half a day and hid in the wild country. They made a suitable blind where they could keep an eye on their surroundings. They drank water and munched on hardtack. They kept a cold camp just in case. Too much had happened in the past weeks to let their guard down.

"It's time for me to return and get the money," John said. "I reckon it'll still be there."

"Don't go, John," Jodi pleaded. "It's only money. We can steal more gold and silver. If you get caught again, we may not be able to get you out. Since you were arrested in El Paso on trumped-up charges, we've been on the run constantly. I've worried myself sick the last weeks. Now that we're all together and alive, why don't we ride for New Mexico? We ain't ever been there. So, they shouldn't know what we look like. Please, John!"

"And leave our money after risking our lives?" Jed asked incredulously.

"When Marshal Thorn had me in his custody, you didn't hold back. You came right after me, even though we had just robbed a bank. You must have thought I was more important than money or even a posse." Jodi said, realizing Jed really did love her.

It sure took some doing for him to show it, but now it was clear. He had risked everything to save her from Marshal Thorn. Luckily, they didn't have to kill the marshal. All three of them appeared to have escaped without a scratch. Sure, Jodi must be collecting some mental baggage by now but, if she lived with Jed, that would be a way of life until they reached California and absolute freedom.

First, John followed Jesse and his men's trails to ensure they weren't going the same way this time. After a day's ride, he confirmed they had fled north. They had successfully robbed the Austin bank at the edge of town, defeated the posse and escaped.

Hearing they were free of the chaos and pandemonium that followed the James Gang was a relief. Jodi would be happy if she never saw the James Gang again. Jesse still scared the daylights out of her. She figured most women would be afraid of him, too, and a majority of men.

CHAPTER 14

BANK ROBBERIES

BACK AT THE BANK ON THE EDGE OF TOWN
MINUTES BEFORE

"THIS BETTER HAPPEN QUICK," MARSHAL HARD TALK SAID.
"I don't know how long these gunmen will hold out
before striking out on their own to collect the bounty
money. Half our posse are gunslingers."

"You best be careful what ya ask for," Sheriff Hader
said. "You just might get it."

As if on cue, the James Gang stormed into town from
the other end of the street, right by the bank they
intended to rob. Of course, they immediately saw the
lawmen trying to hide, but they had poor cover. Jesse
was headstrong, and even when it was best to retreat, he
rode on and fought. He was like a river rat in a corner.
Odds or numbers never deterred him. He had seen
Bloody Bill Anderson overcome eight to one odds. He
conquered because of his willingness to kill. There was
never any doubt or hesitation. Second thoughts only got
in the way. If guards or other soldiers blocked the objec-

tive, they simply ran them over. The lawmen would be no different for the James Gang. They knew they wouldn't be as hard as the men they fought in the war.

Ten men tried to hide in a place with few spots for cover. The savings and loan was small but was said to hold a large payroll. That was what the James Gang were told by their friend, who gave them refuge in his barn.

On one side sat an empty corral at the very end of the street. On the other side was an alley and a barber shop. No sooner did the gang show up than the lawmen opened fire. Marshal Talk stood at the front of his posse, giving his men orders. He acted like a general commanding an army.

The James Gang was made up of guerrilla warriors, who were accustomed to battle within city limits. As soon as the first shot was fired, a cacophony of bullets whizzed through the air from both sides. Windows shattered, and the few horses along the street groaned and squealed. Some of them pulled loose and ran for the center of town. The few citizens on the edge of Austin dove for cover or scurried away from the gunbattle being waged right there in the street.

Jesse, Frank, and the Youngers immediately took offensive positions, recklessly charging right at the lawmen. Three of the ten posse members lost their grit, broke ranks and fled as the rest threw lead at the outlaws. Jesse delivered well-placed bullet, one hitting Sheriff Hader in the gut. He dropped his guns, grabbed his belly and doubled over. He fell to the ground as blood pumped from the wound. He bled far too much and far too fast for him to survive the hour. He looked up at the outlaw with hate in the eyes. He knew Jesse James had killed him like countless others.

The Austin law heard the gunfire and cautiously followed the noise. Horses squealed as they, too, were hit by reckless bullets. Men swore and yelled above the din of gunfire.

Marshal Talk stood and sought cover at the edge of the bank's porch. A barrage of bullets splintered the wood on the wall he stood behind. He had never been on the receiving end of such an onslaught of bullets. He pushed his revolver around the corner and fired his gun blindly, without seeing where he was shooting. All he had in mind was killing Jesse James and saving his own bacon. The rest of the posse didn't matter. They served as cannon fodder for the power-seeking lawman.

The barber hid behind the massive chair in his salon. When there was a lull in the firing, he decided to make a break for the center of town. He was so close to the gunfire every window and mirror in the shop was shot out. The striped pole in front was turned by a small air turbine on the top and had a dozen bullets in it. It still spun but squeaked loudly and wobbled oddly on its axis.

He grabbed his bowler hat in one hand so it wouldn't blow off his head and sprinted down the boardwalk. Marshal Talk was startled when he burst out the doors beside the bank and shot him in the back. The barber faceplanted in the dirt with a bullet hole in him the size of a walnut. The exit wound was bigger than a fist. Hard Talk didn't have to look to know he was dead. He immediately realized he had shot a citizen, but he didn't hesitate a second.

He recklessly threw more wild bullets hither and tither hoping one would kill one of the James Gang. So far, not a single outlaw was winged, but two deputies lay dead, the sheriff was mortally injured and three more ran away. Now they were only four against the six infamous outlaws. They stood no chance before the superior skills of the ex-soldiers.

Despite the defense of the posse, the outlaws still intended to rob the bank, law or no law. They had whittled them down to a few men, and nobody was turning back.

"The Austin law will come next," Frank yelled over the din of gunfire. "Let's get the money and scat before they have another posse after us. I doubt these four fools will do much to stop us."

The gunfire from the lawmen diminished enough for Frank and Jesse to bust into the bank while the Younger brothers held the law at bay. The bank manager and tellers were already hiding behind the caged wall riddled with bullets. Their boots crunched on the glass as they headed for the money. The teller's drawers were open, and the key was in the locked cage where the vault's heavy door hung open for the business day.

In minutes, the gang shoved all the cash into white cloth bags and retreated out the door and to the horses Cole Younger held in wait. None of them were impressed with the bullets whizzing by them. The lawmen hadn't hit a target yet.

As soon as Jesse and Frank swung astride their horses, they wheeled them toward the center of town and gigged their flanks. They lunged forward as the James brothers held onto the bags of money. The Youngers provided cover from the rear. Bullets whistled close to their heads but zipped by. Everything happened so fast. it was over in five minutes. In such a short a time, the once-busy end of town was shot full of bullet holes. There wasn't an unbroken glass window in sight.

Jesse's eyes were lit up like a Christmas tree. He was in his element and having the time of his life. What most people would consider nerve-racking and dangerous was his bread and butter. He loved his lifestyle and didn't know another way of life. His brother worried because he knew his behavior one day would get him killed if not them both.

CHAPTER 15

THE GETAWAY

When the James Gang fled toward the center of town Marshal Talk and what deputies were left rushed to mount their horses and took pursuit. The outlaws had successfully robbed the bank even with the posse there to stop them. The lawmen's trap quickly turned into pandemonium.

The outlaws shot their guns off in the air, scattering the locals like a flock of hens fleeing an angry wolf. They lashed their horses to race faster down Main Street toward the other end of town. Just as an Austin posse organized themselves, the James Gang ran right through the middle of them, forcing them to bound like deer for cover. Immediately, the volunteers disbanded. They saw the crazy look on Jesse's face and believed they would die if they mounted any type of pursuit.

The town marshal, Rich Words, breathed a sigh of relief when the James brothers raced out of town, followed by the Youngers. With no posse for support, he could stay in the safety of his town. Words had no aspirations to be any more than the town law. He was glad the posse had fallen apart before they even got after the bank robbers. He knew too well most heroes were dead ones.

Confusion ran through the crowd because nobody was sure if one or two banks had been robbed. Nor was it clear if the James Gang pulled off both bank heists. Puzzled faces filled the accumulating crowd. Somebody said the James Gang was in town, and everybody wanted to see what the infamous outlaws looked like. All they saw was the blur of six riders when they rode past. Most of the spectators dove for cover to keep from getting shot.

Right behind the gang, firing their guns even more recklessly, was what remained of the San Antonio posse. Marshal Hard Talk had left Hader lying on the ground bleeding out. He was utterly obsessed with capturing Jesse and Frank. Nothing else was on his mind. Indeed, safety was not an issue that caused him worry, not for himself or the citizens. All he could think about was seeing his picture on the front page of national newspapers alongside the dead body of Jesse James.

Hard Talk lashed his horse as he gigged its bleeding flanks and he too roared past the crowd with his last three deputies following. He continued to send wild bullets toward the outlaw gang. Many hit buildings and windows along the way. It was a miracle that more civilians were not wounded or killed with the reckless way he and his men used their guns. None of their shots came near to hitting a single outlaw, although they did leave the town full of holes from one end of Main Street to the other.

JED AND JODI another day alone. It would take John a half day to make sure which way the James Gang went and another half day to get back. They would be spending the night alone for the first time since before the trouble in El Paso. To Jodi, it seemed they never got any quality time together.

As Jodi said, getting in touch with his feelings wasn't something Jed relished. He knew there was right and wrong. In the middle, society's criers and whiners existed. They were citizens who had inherited the luxury and safety of freedom. People like John, because he was Black, and Jed, because he was a notorious Rebel soldier, never knew anything about freedom before. She wondered if they would really reach California in the end like she and Uncle John hoped and prayed.

Like John, Jodi still had at least a little faith in hope. She knew what Jed thought about it. He felt if there was hope, disappointment lurked nearby to shatter high expectations. He learned to never expect squat.

The day Jodi saw hope return to Jed's eyes was the day she knew she had won him over completely. Until then, she knew there always would be that barrier to break to reach his soul.

The sun set and blushed the sky in a prism of colors. A blanket of stars rolled across the heavens to the distant horizon. Lightning bugs danced their nightly chorus, flashing and then vanishing into the dark.

The small fire encouraged them to snuggle together to keep the desert chill off. A series of falling stars streaked across the sky as they sat and watched the wonders of nature in a comfortable silence.

Jodi took Jed's hand, closed her eyes, and made a wish. Coal stared at the falling stars without comment.

Coyotes howled at the moon and called out to each other. They shared a cup of heavily laced coffee. They didn't want to sleep yet and have their time alone together fly by too quickly. They sat late into the night, snuggling, and whispering breathlessly into each other's ears.

Jodi's neck was long and delicate. Under that rough Texas cowgirl's facade was a sensitive woman. When Jed touched her, it felt like an electric shock went through her body. When he embraced her, she melted in his arms. She purred like a cat as she curled up with Jed and spooned under the covers. Eventually they fell into a satisfying sleep.

They both felt like they were at the bottom of a deep dark well leaving them in a satisfying slumber. For a few hours they thought of nothing but each other. They forgot about the war and the posse. The James Gang even slipped from their minds as they focused their attention on each other.

CHAPTER 16

STARLIT NIGHTS

By the time John Washington returned to camp it was the end of the second day. Of course, Jed didn't worry about his partner. When he was traveling alone, John was like a ghost. He shifted between the shadows and difficult places to see. So Jed and Jodi had time to make up, soothe each other's wounds and make plans to head west. They had had one of those special nights that occurred once in a blue moon.

This time the moon was a bright white. The sky was so clear they could see the lunar craters. It looked like a big piece of round cheese. That night they slept arm in arm in a deep peaceful sleep. The following morning Jodi was up before Jed and making some frying pan biscuits and fried pork for breakfast.

Jed sat up and smiled. He rubbed the sleep away with the heels of his hands and breathed in the scent of sizzling bacon. The skillet popped and cracked. He raked his fingers through his hair and stretched his arms. When he sniffed the air, it was scented with the aroma of freshly perked coffee. It was rare Jodi had the opportunity to cook breakfast for Jed, especially when they were on the run. He pulled his suspenders over his shoulders and slipped into a plaid shirt.

His eyes danced with delight. Jodi had learned to see the telltale signs of anger, disappointment and even the occasional moment of joy his eyes could not hide. That was where Jed showed his feelings. Sometimes his secrets were there to see, too.

It was a long way away from the face he made when he was after Marshal Thorn for snatching his girl. Even though it just happened, it already seemed like a long time ago. When she saw Jed in his ultimate state of anger, it was a thing of awe and foreboding. She didn't care to see it again, but something told her their lives wouldn't allow it to remain hidden forever inside this violent man.

"Mornin' darlin'," Jed said. He even sort of smiled.

Jodi grinned from ear to ear. Her white teeth stood like rows of corn. She grinned so wide her wisdom teeth sparkled.

"Mornin' to you, honeybunch. Come on, get your biscuits while they're hot or they won't be nearly as good. I even got a tin of grape jam to go with breakfast," she said.

Jed sat on a horse blanket and stared into the distance. He felt so comfortable, he had forgotten to look for danger. Usually, as soon as he or John opened their eyes, they scanned their surroundings for enemies or traces of the presence of Indians. If a man wanted to stay alive, he had to stay sharp. On this day, he had not only slept in but let his guard down for just a moment.

He made a mental note to remember the rules of the

game in the future. You can act like everything is normal all you want but that doesn't mean it's true.

"Whatcha wanna do today?" Jodi asked. "We don't have a thing to do but whatever tickles our fancy."

The obvious happened and they stayed in their little camp all day. The horses grazed nearby as hawks circled in the sky above looking for small prey. Cicadas and crickets fought for the right to make more noise than the other, but Jed and Jodi hardly noticed. Soon the sun was a couple of hours from the horizon and sure enough a silhouette was riding their way.

"Whatcha doin' comin' from the west?" Jed asked. "I thought the boys would go north.

"They headed west first then turned north," John said as he stepped down from his horse and began to remove the saddle. When he pulled the bridle off, the animal turned and joined the other horses grazing in the shade.

"I followed 'em till they were far enough away so they ain't dangerous for us. They have fresh horses and should be heading home. I rode west for a few hours to make sure they didn't turn back and go that way. There was no sign of 'em, though. So, I reckon we can rest easy and head west like we planned."

John took a seat as Jodi filled a tin pie pan with pork and beans. She broke open three biscuits and used a spoon to spread sweet grape jam over both sides and passed them to John. Washington didn't talk again until he wiped the pan dry with the last of the morning biscuits.

"How much money have we got?" Jed asked Jodi. She had taken on the job of keeping track of their money.

"We've got plenty for now," Jodi replied. "I reckon about three hundred dollars."

"And all that money we stole from the Wells Fargo Bank is back there under the building?" John huffed. "I wonder if anybody found it yet?"

"If the coyotes ain't dragged it away." Jodi smiled. "There's plenty more where that money came from. I reckon they have banks in New Mexico, don't they? Whatcha worrin' about, boys?"

She knew it rubbed them wrong leaving the bullion from the heist, but it was the money or their lives as far as she could see. Things were getting too tight to take any more chances. They had nearly lost John once to the court in El Paso and that ornery racist Judge Axel Black. After that everything went to hell.

She had no intention of letting the same thing happen again. It was those James boys who brought the heat after the hearing. Even if Jesse did save John's life, she hoped they never ran into them again.

"I wonder if Bob Younger's eye ever straightened back out." Jed smiled. "He was cruisin' for a beating, and he bit off more than he could chew. I never shy away from givin' a bully a good dose of their own medicine. Bob's been mouthin' off for too darn long. It was time for it to stop."

"I reckon you stopped him pretty good," John said and laughed. "The doc had to wire his mouth shut to keep his jaw from fallin' off. You can hardly understand what he's says now."

"There wasn't nothin' but stupid comin' out of his mouth anyway. The world is a better place now," Jed joked.

"Oh, you stopped him all right," Jodi said and snickered. "With that eye of his all askew, I doubt he could hit the side of a barn with a scattergun."

That night they all dreamed of California. John had been dreaming of San Francisco even back when he was a regular slave and not an indentured soldier. Even though his freedom now was limited, he made do with what he had. He didn't answer to anyone and went where he wanted. He even managed to acquire two good friends in his chaotic travels. What more could a man in his position ask of life? Jed and Jodi were the only family he had left, other than his brother. He was unsure if he had survived.

Jodi dreamed the same dream she had dreamed for weeks. She envisioned herself and Jed walking down a Pacific beach along the California coast. They walked hand in hand as the sun set in the west over the vast body of water.

Even Jed dreamed of the West Coast, but in his own way. He was hunting in the northern forests for elk and bear. For some reason he felt at ease in the forest. After the hunt, he saw himself head toward a log cabin. A trail of smoke squirreled out of the chimney. Laundry festooned beside the cabin as a blonde woman hung clothing to dry.

In his dream, she turned his way, and he could see the love and kindness in her eyes. He realized that maybe there was a future somewhere far ahead for them. California could just be the place they would find peace. A smidgen of hope snuck into Jed's dream. It was something he had shunned for a long time. For the first time in years, he dreamed about a thing called hope.

A LOOK AT:
ABANDONED (BENJIE WILLOW THE ORPHAN1)

A massacre stole everything—the trail to El Paso might give him a reason to keep going…

Fourteen-year-old Benjie Willow should've died with the rest of his family. Hidden in a water well as Comanche raiders swept through his ranch on the Red River, he emerged into a world he no longer recognized—alone, grieving, and hunted.

When seasoned frontiersman Malvo Tanner and the quiet Choctaw warrior Chito-Oche spot smoke on the horizon, they don't expect to find a terrified boy as the only survivor. Taking Benjie in, they set off for El Paso, dragging him through lawless lands where danger rides faster than justice…and the past haunts every mile.

But the West isn't kind to orphans, and as Benjie struggles to find his place in this brutal new world, he'll have to learn what it means to survive…not just in body, but in spirit.

Will the trail harden him into something unrecognizable…or forge a future he never dared to imagine?

AVAILABLE SEPTEMBER 2025

ABOUT THE AUTHOR

 Born in 1886 in Southern Ohio, Ash Lingam grew crops, raised cattle, and doted on the young boy. Ash's family was among the early settlers in pre-Revolutionary America. He has traced his lineage back to around 1746 when his ancestors immigrated from Europe to the aspiring American Colonies.

A retired marketing executive, Ash devotes his spare time to training police dogs and writing novels. He has found his niche in the Western, historical fiction, and adventure genres. With his vast vault of experience, he never runs out of sources for new stories. He has lived in eleven different countries and worked in a total of forty-six to date, Ash has written approximately 130 novels, short stories, and poems. More than one hundred of his eclectic titles help the American frontier come alive for his readers.

https://www.ashlingam.com/